No Reprieve

Ravenswood Crime Series

Tony Millington

City Stone Publishing

ISBN (paperback): 978-1-915399-19-9
ISBN (ePUB): 978-1-915399-20-5

A CIP catalogue record for this book is available from the British Library.

Tony Millington | www.facebook.com/TonyMillingtonAuthor

City Stone Publishing | www.citystonepublishing.com

First printed: May 2018
Second edition: February 2022
Third edition: June 2023

To Mum

Joan Millington
1939-2023

CHAPTER ONE

Tuesday Night 11.30 p.m.

It was past kicking out time at The Dragon's Den. Ronald Freeman downed the dregs of his last pint and said goodnight to the landlord of his local. He had been cheering on their pool team, who had beaten The King's Head 7-2 in the local league.

The last to leave, having consumed far too much alcohol, he staggered through the back door of the pub towards the car park. It had been raining most of the evening, so he zig-zagged across the tarmac, trying to avoid the rain-filled potholes.

Freeman lit a cigarette, keeping it in his mouth as he reached for the car door and fumbled for the keys in his trousers pocket, dropping them on the ground, and swearing under his breath. Leaning over, he grabbed them before opening the door of the battered silver VW Passat, which he had abandoned haphazardly next to a wall at the back of the car park. With the cigarette still hanging from his mouth, Freeman slid into the driver's seat and started the engine, doing the seatbelt up.

There was a knock on the window. Puzzled, he wound down the window and glared through the cigarette smoke and rain mist to see a human form standing by his car.

'Mr Ronald Freeman?' the stranger asked.

'Yes? Who the fuck wants to know?' Freeman snarled.

'This is for Fredrick Mason,' Colin Littlewood said calmly. He fired twice. The back of Freeman's head exploded as the bullets entered through the forehead, showering the inside of the car with pieces of skull and brain matter. He slumped in the seat, held in place only by his seat belt.

Colin Littlewood knew where Freeman would be that night. He had been following him for over a week, following at a safe distance to work out the best time and place to kill Freeman. Littlewood had surveyed the car park and noted the ill-lit corners at the back where the bins were. Would Freeman park there? Littlewood figured he would, as the car park usually was full by the time Freeman arrived at the pub. It had made it all too easy, he thought. It had been an excellent place to wait in the shadows, near the industrial bins.

So, he'd waited in the perfect spot to put a bullet in Freeman's head. Yes, it stank, but it would be worth it. If anyone saw him there and asked, he was just looking for his dog. As Littlewood slipped away unnoticed, he had mixed feelings about his now heavy and drenched donkey coat. But, he remembered, it had the perfect pockets to hide a gun.

Now walking away nonchalantly past the pub, he couldn't suppress his euphoria. 'One down,' he said and smiled.

Revenge was sweet.

—

It was nearly midnight. Terry Watson yawned. He turned off the bedside lights when the "War of the Worlds" theme music blared from his phone.

His wife, Sally, sat up and scowled at him. 'Who could ring at this time of night?' she asked sarcastically.

Terry thought about cracking a joke, but decided against it. He picked up the phone from the bedside table. 'I'll be outside in five,' he heard, as expected, the voice of his friend and colleague, Detective Sergeant Keith Monteith.

'Are you in the car already?' Watson asked. 'Where's the fire?'

'It's a shooting, guv,' Monteith responded.

'I'll be waiting.' Watson could hear the spinning of the car wheels.

Watson quickly threw back on the day's clothes as Sally looked on. He checked he had everything, including his police ID, warrant card, and radio.

'Is it really necessary?' Sally asked, Bugs Bunny grinning at him from her nightshirt. 'You know I hate it when you go off in the middle of the night.' Do you have to go?'

'After fifteen years of marriage, you still ask me that.' Watson turned when he reached the top of the stairs and kissed her.

'Because I care, you silly sod,' Sally sighed loudly, taking one last cuddle and kiss before he walked down the stairs.

'Love you, Sally,' he called as he opened the front door.

Outside, Monteith was already waiting in his BMW.

—

Sally watched him go out of the door and heard him lock it from the front. She dreaded to think what kind of risk he was going to face. What if one day she got the call, or the visit, that every wife feared? The one that meant he wouldn't be coming home?

'Where's daddy going?' A sleepy voice called out from one bedroom.

Sally opened the door. Six-year-old Rachael was sitting up in bed. 'He has to go into work, little miss, and you should be asleep. Did we wake you?' Sally entered the room and tucked her daughter back into bed.

'I heard Dad's phone going off and both of you talking,' Rachael said as she lay back down and rubbed her closing eyes.

'He will be back soon, darling. Now I think we should both try to get some sleep.' She kissed her daughter on the forehead. 'Goodnight sweetie.'

The little girl, half asleep, cuddled up to her favourite teddy bear, dressed as a policeman. 'Night Mum.'

Sally checked on their other two children, Simon and Jason, before returning to an empty bed. She hoped her husband would be safe.

***

As Watson shut and locked the front door, Monteith was already outside, waiting. His car's headlights showed a fine rain was still falling. Watson jumped into the passenger seat.

'Got out alive then?' Monteith said, as he floored the BMW.

'Yes. Sally was fine. Wasn't Katie?'

'I think the last thing I heard her mumble beneath the duvet was "piss off and save the world then",' Monteith laughed.

Ravenswood was a city with a population of around 250,000. Much like other cities, it had newly built estates you'd love to live in, but couldn't afford, areas you wouldn't live even if someone paid you, and areas that were somewhere in the middle.

Detective Chief Inspector Watson and DS Monteith had been in the Ravenswood police force for the last five years. They'd gone to school together and had been friends since as well as having been each other's best man.

Reaching the crime scene in the city's Bankside, Monteith parked up on the street in front of The Dragon's Den. Uniform had secured the area; the crime scene tape went across the gateway at the side of the pub. Floodlights illuminated the car park at the rear, reaching into the areas the security light could not. A forensics tent had been erected to cover the car from onlookers and prevent any potential contamination of evidence. Under the tent, the forensics investigators were carefully going over a VW Passat with its driver's door open.

As they walked past, Watson and Monteith could glimpse through the flap in the tent; the body inside had almost no head left. Not a pretty sight.

'Nice,' Monteith exclaimed sarcastically.

Detective Constable Karl Lorimer greeted them and led them into the pub via the back door, along a corridor and past the toilets into the main part of the pub. It was split into two, with the bar in the middle serving both sides. One was the lounge area, made into a cosy snug, with soft furnishings and low lighting. It had a well-worn patterned carpet on the floor. The walls had flowered wallpaper on them, with wall lights spaced out around the room. An open fireplace with a large wooden-framed mirror took pride of place along the longest wall.

Pictures of the countryside spaced out around the walls. There were half a dozen easy armchairs around small tables, and a couple beside the fire and under the front-facing window. Barstools and the normal dark wooden laminated tables and wheel backed chairs made up the rest of the seating. The restaurant and the kitchen area were accessible through a door at the far end of the room.

The other side was a games area. It wasn't quite spit and sawdust, but not far off. There were large, dirty, cream-coloured tiles on the floor. The walls and ceiling were stained dirty nicotine yellow, remnants from when smoking was still allowed indoors. On the walls were the obligatory two pictures of dressed-up dogs playing pool and cards. Two large windows looked out on the street outside. At the far end of the room was a blue baize coloured pool table, along with a dartboard. A Wurlitzer jukebox stood next to the corridor which led out to the toilets and back door. The lighting came from three shaded lights in the ceiling and two wall lights.

The landlord, Mr Preston, sat at the bar in the spit and sawdust side, nursing a glass of whisky.

'He's given us a name of the victim, a Ronald Freeman,' DC Lorimer said. 'But nothing else.'

'Ok, thank you, Karl.' Watson went over to the landlord, introduced himself, and sat down on a barstool.

'What can you tell us, Mr Preston?' Watson asked gently,

'I'd just shown Ronald out of the door and said good night. I locked up and then a couple of minutes later I heard two bangs.'

Mr Preston paused and gulped down his large whisky in one.

'I thought his was having trouble with his car, backfiring. I can't remember how many times I said he should get a better one, but he wouldn't listen. I unlocked and went out of the door, and saw...'

With that, he collapsed in tears, his body and shoulders heaving as the shock of the night hit him. Watson leaned over, placed a hand on his shoulder, and quietly thanked him, before getting up and strolling over to Monteith, near the jukebox.

'We won't get much out of him tonight,' Watson said, looking back at Mr Preston. 'Let's see what we can find outside.'

Back out in the car park, the rain had thankfully stopped. Both tried to do a quickstep around the water-filled potholes. Watson failed and his right foot went straight into one. 'Bollocks!' he shouted, shaking his foot to get the water off.

'Good job there are floodlights on, or you would have got both feet wet!' Monteith laughed.

The police pathologist James Macintosh, or Mac the Knife, as they called him, had arrived and was in the tent, studying Ronald Freeman's body.

'Hi Mac, what we got?' asked Watson.

'A bloody mess, that's what,' Mac answered. 'Why can't killers just put the bullets into the body instead of having to blow a person's brains half out? Would make my job a lot easier. I will have to pick this car apart to get the rest of this head.'

'But you love it, don't you, Mac?' grinned Monteith.

'Yes, great fun trying to do a skull jigsaw, then finding out there is a piece missing.' Mac had a big grin of his own.

'The landlord said he heard two bangs,' DCI Watson interjected.

'Yes... that would cause this mess. Not sure about the calibre until we find the bullets. Will let you know when I get him back to the lab.'

'Have you found any identification?'

'There's a wallet here with a driving licence belonging to Ronald Freeman.' Mac handed it over in a clear evidence bag to Watson.

'That name ties in with what the landlord said. Ok Mac, seems that you have everything under control here. See you back at the morgue when you're ready for the autopsy.' With that, they left Mac and his team to their job.

Wednesday Night 12:07 a.m.

Littlewood parked his car on the drive next to his daughter's.

Opening the front door of his terrace house, and with one last glance around to make sure nobody had seen him, he entered and locked it behind him. He put his wet donkey jacket on the hanger behind the door. Satisfied with his night's work, he walked into the front room. His daughter Susan was sitting on the sofa with her legs tucked up, watching a film on Netflix. She looked up as he entered.

'Enjoy your evening?' she said, smiling.

'Yes, very,' he replied, leaning over her and kissing her forehead. He watched the film she had on. *One Flew Over the Cuckoo's Nest.* He had seen it more times than he cared to remember.

'I think I'll go up. See you in the morning, sweetheart.'

Susan turned her head towards him. 'Night, Dad.'

Littlewood removed the gun from his coat and took it upstairs to his bedroom. Opening his wardrobe, he knelt down and pulled out an old rucksack tucked away in the back. He put the gun deep inside the rucksack and removed a red-bound book. Opening it, and with the pen attached, he put a line through the first name on the list: Ronald Freeman.

***

Detective Superintendent Kenneth Crompton had over twenty years of policing behind him. He had climbed up through the ranks the traditional way and was big in stature, both in build and reputation. Always called a spade a spade and did not like people bullshitting him, but there to help anyone in need.

At one a.m., he was still sitting behind his large wooden desk in his glass-walled office. When Watson and Monteith arrived back, he was on the phone but waved them in.

'The press office is looking for a heads up. What have we got?' Crompton asked after finishing his call.

Watson and Monteith, looking exhausted, sat down in the leather backed chairs on the other side of his desk.

Watson began. 'We've just got back from the shooting at The Dragon's Den. White male shot in his car in the pub's car park at the back, around 11.30 p.m. last night. The landlord said after locking up he heard two loud bangs. He ran out into the car park and found the man's lifeless body strapped into the driver's seat.'

'Did he know the victim?'

'The name he has given is the same as on the victim's driving licence. Ronald Freeman.'

Crompton sat bolt upright in his chair. 'What? Who?' The colour drained from his face.

'The victim is Ronald Freeman,' Watson repeated.

'Are you all right, sir?' Monteith pitched in. 'You look like you've seen a ghost.'

Crompton rose out of his chair and went to his cabinet, opened the bottom drawer, and pulled out a bottle of whisky. He poured two shots and sat back down; his face ashen.

'Ronald Freeman is a blast from the past. One of my first cases as a detective.' Crompton took a swig of his whisky.

'He was jailed for the manslaughter of a shop owner, Fred Mason, fifteen years ago. Everyone working the case said it should have been murder. He went to rob the place with a sawn-off shotgun. Mason did not give in and tackled him. The gun went off in the struggle. Mason died from his wounds a few days later.'

Crompton paused, deep in thought. He sighed. His voice was barely above a whisper.

'Until you said his name, I didn't know they had released him, never mind he was back in the city.'

Crompton looked shaken, as if a ghost had walked on his grave. He finished his drink, his hand tightly gripping the glass.

'Boss, are you ok?' Watson looked concerned.

'Yes, yes. Go home, and get some rest. Come back fresh in the morning.'

'You're sure?' Watson asked.

Crompton waved his hand dismissively. 'Yes, go on. I've still got things to do.'

As they left, Crompton stood by the window looking down at the bright lights of the city centre. Only one question was on his mind. *Why? Why now?*

CHAPTER TWO

Wednesday Morning

WATSON ARRIVED AT THE police station, just in time for the 9.30 a.m. briefing. Pathologist James Macintosh had come in to present his initial findings, and DSI Crompton was holding court in his office. Strong coffee and bacon rolls from the cafe down the street were the order of the morning after their brief night.

Crompton's clothes were crumpled; it looked like he'd not been home at all.

'Ok folks, let's get started. Mac, your findings, please.'

'I've not done a full post mortem yet, but it's safe to say Ronald Freeman was shot at point blank range, through the head. In through the forehead and out the back. The two holes in the forehead suggest the killer was outside the car and fired down through the driver's window. What's left of the bullets recovered from the car suggests they were 9mm. Forensics were still there completing their search of the car and the car park when I left with Mr Freeman around 2 a.m.'

'Thanks Mac,' Crompton said, wiping his mouth with a paper napkin after finishing his bacon roll, and throwing it in the bin.

'We need to find out if the killer was in the pub with Freeman, waited until he left and shot him, or if the killer was already waiting outside. Watson, why don't you go back and see if the landlord is up to answering any more questions, please. We need to know who visited the pub last night. Did anybody confront Freeman whilst he was in there? Did he piss anyone off during the evening? I'll get uniform to carry out door-to-door enquiries in the area this morning.'

Watson put his coffee down on the desk on Crompton's spotless desk, unaware of his superintendent's indignant look. 'Boss, before we go, you said last night you knew Freeman and remembered why he got put away. Can you enlighten us?'

Crompton leaned back in his chair and gathered himself, struggling with his thoughts. 'I had been promoted to detective about two months earlier, and this was my first big case. Freeman entered Fred Mason's newsagent in the evening with a shotgun to rob it. He brandished the gun at the young girl behind the counter, Mason's daughter, and demanded the money from the till. Fred Mason was stacking shelves in the shop, and when he heard Freeman, he came out and confronted him. Mason made a lunge for the gun to protect his daughter. During the struggle, the gun went off. Mason suffered serious wounds to his chest and died in hospital two days later. Freeman ran out of the shop, taking nothing. He'd been in prison before but, up to that evening, only for petty theft. Mason's daughter identified him from mug shots.'

Crompton took a slurp of his coffee. 'We were confident he would get put away for murder, but to our horror, his lawyers were so good the jury only convicted him of manslaughter. He got sixteen years in Craythorn Prison. That was twelve years ago. That's why I was stunned he was out.'

The room fell silent.

In a low voice, Watson said, 'Boss, don't worry, we will catch the killer.'

Crompton looked up with a vacant stare and nodded slowly.

Walking out, Watson signalled for Monteith to follow him. 'Come on, let's go.'

'He's still shook up over this Freeman shooting,' Watson commented as they were making their way through the busy traffic to The Dragon's Den.

'I bet it's nothing, guv. It's because, as he said, Freeman was his first case.' Monteith grinned. 'We all can remember our first cases when we joined. It was part of the thrill back then. Now they all seem to roll into one another. Ours was that drug bust at the cannabis factory. I remember still being high on the fumes the plants gave off the next day. The clearance team had to do it in twenty-minute shifts because there were so many plants and the smell they gave off affected them so much.'

'Yes, I remember, but I don't know. I think there's something more to this.' Watson sounded unsure.

'You're reading too much into it, guv, lighten up.' With that, Monteith flattened the accelerator.

'Slow down, slow down you, idiot. I don't want to end up on Mac's table just yet,' Watson shouted, grabbing onto the sides of his seat.

———

When they arrived at the Dragon's Den, they found the press already present, assembled behind the tape, which had been strung up across the end of the road.

They hoped it wouldn't be too much of a pain for the morning travellers, as the pub was on a bus route.

Once they were let through, Monteith had to park his car on the road as crime scene tape was still across the gate leading to the car park. They showed their badges to the officer on the gate and ducked under the tape. As they walked around the side of the pub into the car park, forensics were packing away their gear into a white-panelled van.

'They look like beings from another planet when they're in all of their paper hazmat suits,' Watson commented.

'You've been watching too many sci-fi programs,' Monteith joked back.

'I'm glad someone has something to laugh about,' a woman shouted at them. She was standing by the pub's back door, smoking. A small stout woman dressed in a knee-length black skirt, patterned blouse and thin cardigan.

'I'm sorry, madam, that was bad taste,' said Monteith apologetically. 'My name is Detective Sergeant Monteith, and this is Detective Chief Inspector Watson.'

The woman threw them an indignant glance. 'I know who you are. I saw you last night. I'm Elizabeth Preston, follow me.' She put her cigarette out on the wall and led them through the door, taking them into the main area of the pub.

The cleaners were going about their business as the three of them sat at a table in the lounge area.

'Is your husband around, Mrs Preston? We would like to ask him a few more questions about what happened last night,' Watson asked.

'I'm sorry, he is asleep. After you left, the doctor came and gave him a sedative. Any questions you have, I can help with,' Elizabeth said resolutely.

Watson glanced at Monteith as if to say that's us told, before asking, 'Where were you last night when Ronald Freeman was killed?'

'Murdered, Chief Inspector. Don't you forget that,' Elizabeth scowled. 'I was upstairs. I'd put our two children to bed an hour before and stayed up there until... you know what. I heard two loud bangs and went to look out of the window overlooking the car park. Peter, my husband, came running out from the back door. He went across to Ronald's car and looked through the window, then threw up by the wall. He shouted up to call the police, which I did.'

'Did you see anybody else in the car park?'

'No,' Elizabeth paused, 'But, I didn't think about it until now. I thought I saw the gate at the far end of the car park swing shut before Peter came out.'

'Where does that gate lead to?' Watson asked, while Monteith was jotting everything down.

'There is a large pathway which runs behind us and the other terrace houses on this side of the street. The refuse lorries and some delivery vans use it.'

'When you went upstairs, can you remember who was down here in the bar, Mrs Preston?'

'Only Peter, Ronald and two other regulars who only live across the street; they would have gone out the front door. We'd a pool match earlier in the evening, but they'd all left by the time Peter had locked up.'

A cleaner came into the lounge and started to polish the tables.

'June, can you hang on till we've finished?' Elizabeth asked tersely.

'Oh, sorry, I didn't see you there.' the cleaner replied as she picked up her bucket and went back out.

'Was Ronald a regular in the pub?' Monteith picked up the questioning.

'Yes, three or four times a week he comes in.' She paused. 'Came in.'

'Always the same days each week?' Watson asked.

'Yes, when the pool or darts teams are playing at home. He didn't play, but he liked to cheer them on.'

Watson and Monteith glanced again at each other.

Mrs Preston noticed and sat up straight.

'Do you think someone planned this? Knew he would be here?' Her eyes were wide open with fright.

'Well, we don't know yet. We have only just started the investigation. Did anyone cause him any trouble in here last night?' Watson tried to recover the situation.

'No,' Mrs Preston said forcefully. 'Now leave. Get out and catch the bastard who killed him.' With that, she got up and turned away. She stared through the front window, arms folded, a look of despair on her face as tears started to flow.

Watson and Monteith got up and made their way to the door. Watson stopped and said, 'One last question, Mrs Preston. The address on his driver's licence is on the other side of town. Why did he make this pub his local?'

Elizabeth turned back to them. She looked confused. 'Don't you know? Ronald Freeman was my brother.'

Wednesday Afternoon

Littlewood was back on the move. He wanted to check on the next person on his list. Jackson Davis.

Of all the people he had marked down, this one made his skin crawl and his blood boil. Jackson had tortured and killed two prostitutes twenty-five years ago. He might have served his time, but Littlewood was not prepared to let this murderer go unpunished. He had been watching Davis for about a week now, working out his routines.

Today, as always, Jackson had taken his Alsatian for a walk in the park across the road from his house. Littlewood parked his red Skoda Fabia on a nearby street, locked it and went into the park.

He wandered around for a couple of minutes, taking in the afternoon sun before sitting on a bench, not too close to Davis, but close enough to watch him. He picked up a newspaper which had been left. *A nice disguise*, he thought as he leaved through the pages.

The park was not one of the biggest in the city. It had big green spaces with pathways crisscrossing; flower beds were in full bloom, and trees lined the pathways around the edge. Mothers with small children were making the most of the weather, getting out of the house with their kids for some fresh air before they went crazy.

Davis was there talking to the youngsters using the gym equipment, teaching them the best way of doing dips and pull-ups on the bars. Davis may have been sixty-two, but he still carried a big physical presence. Littlewood could visualise him trying to keep fit in the prison's gym, even though he didn't approve of prisons having things like that.

Prison was a punishment and shouldn't be a holiday camp, he pondered. He had read in some on-line newspaper article that most prisons provided satellite TV and computer games for their guests at Her Majesty's pleasure. One they said had a state-of-the art gym. It angered Littlewood. Over twenty pounds a month for Mr Law-Abiding Joe Bloggs on the outside, free for the scum on the inside. A complete waste of taxpayers' money, he thought grimly.

After about thirty minutes of watching and reviewing his surroundings, Littlewood saw all he needed to. This takeout would be a lot harder than Freeman. More in-depth planning was needed, and the park was not the place to do it. He would have loved to walk over to Davis and pulled the trigger on him there and then, but that was not the way. He wanted to savour Davis' demise, wanted to put him through the same horrors the prostitutes suffered.

Returning to his car, he made notes in his red book, and left to plan Davis' demise.

***

Jackson Davis had clocked the loner on the bench.

A single man on his own, looking so far out of place in a park full of mothers and children, dog walkers, and teenagers. All he needed was a sign around his neck saying "loser".

He couldn't care less who he was, a father trying to get a glimpse of his children after a divorce, the police doing undercover surveillance on somebody. Maybe him for all he knew. A looney fan trying to get close to him. They existed. There were other jailbirds he was in with who received so-called fan mail from the public. Pen pals, they called it. He couldn't work out who had less morals, the ones in jail or the ones that sent the letters.

Davis let the loner leave first, and then he said his goodbyes to the teenagers at the gym equipment. As he was going out of the gate, he put his dog's poo in the doggie bin. He crossed the road with his Alsatian by his side and up his gravel drive, where his black Toyota RAV4 was parked.

He let his dog off the lead once they got into the house. The dog's tail wagged hard, his nose to the floor until he got to his water bowl for a long drink. Davis made his way up the carpeted stairs to his bedroom, opened the glass-fronted wardrobe and flicked through his stylish shirts. He smiled as he picked out his outfit for the evening's entertainment. Tonight, he would go out on the town and have fun. His kind of fun.

Back at the police station, Watson gathered everyone around the large white board attached to the wall which held all the information on the case. It wasn't much, other than the pictures of Ronald Freeman's body, slumped in the car. Gruesome, that it was. Pictures of some things of interest the forensics team found in the car park, and pictures of what was left of the bullets. That was all.

'What else do we have?' DSI Crompton said as he sat at the edge of a desk in the main office area.

'The door to door came up with nothing. Nobody was around that time of night,' Lorimer said, sitting at his desk, looking at his notes. 'One or two said they heard loud bangs or something, but couldn't see anything when they looked out of their windows. The alleyway at the back of the houses is dimly lit and the locals don't use it in the evening or at night.'

Crompton nodded and turned to Watson. 'Did you get anything from Mr Preston?'

'We didn't see Mr Preston,' Watson started. 'But we spoke to his wife, Elizabeth. She said she was Ronald's sister.' Watson scrutinised his boss' face. Nothing.

'And?' Crompton pressed. He got off the desk and paced around, waiting for answers.

'And she said Ronald came in three or four times a week. No problems with other customers. Nobody came in and caused him trouble. She may have seen the back gate open and close, but she cannot be certain. There could be hundreds of fingerprints on there.'

'So, we have nothing from the crime scene, right?' Crompton's frustration was evident. Everyone in the room went quiet and looked down to avoid catching his eye. Crompton stopped pacing.

'Right, you lot, let's check on who his cellmates were in Craythorn. Are any of them out yet? Has he kept in contact with anybody? Check his address.'

'The address on his driver's licence is in Thelwell,' Monteith said.

'Right, Watson, take Monteith and see what you find. Go.' With that, Crompton stormed back into his office and slammed the door shut. The door shook as the rest of the room exchanged glances.

Lorimer slowly shook his head. 'Well, that told us. Is he always like that?'

'Only on good days,' Monteith laughed.

'Remind me not to be around on his bad days. I'll wear my riot gear if I am.'

Watson and Monteith walked back to their desks.

'What the hell are you playing at, guv?' Monteith hissed over the desk divider. 'I saw you look straight at the boss when you said that about Freeman's sister.'

Watson picked up his jacket from the back of his chair. 'There is something the boss is not telling us, I'm sure.'

'You really believe he's holding something back? Sorry, guv, but you're nuts.' Monteith was pointing his finger in Watson's direction.

'Yes, I do, but I don't know what yet.' With that, he walked out.

Monteith grabbed his car keys off the desk and made for the door. 'Come on, I don't want to spend a minute longer than I need to in Thelwell. Not in my car.'

Thelwell wasn't the best part of Ravenswood. In fact, it was one of the worst areas. It was the biggest of the original council estates built when the city undertook redevelopment in the sixties. The council put up the normal street sign "Welcome to Thelwell". One of the local ingenious Van Goghs with his spray paint changed it to "Welcome to ~~Thelwell~~ HELL".

This was where most of the illegal activity in the city took place. You wanted drugs; you got them here. If you were looking for stolen property, chances are you would find it here. Stolen cars were usually dumped here, either burnt out after the joy riders had finished with them, or being welded to another car to make a cut and shut.

The address they had for Freeman turned out to be a hostel on the edge of Thelwell. Watson grinned, he could see Monteith's worry about his pride and joy as he pulled into the small car park at the front. A low wall, which had seen better days, ran along the length of the car park.

They slowly got out, looking around carefully, spotting the local look outs for the gangs and ruling families in the area, kids, who had congregated on the street corner in front of a small newsagent.

'Let's make this quick. I don't want to come out and find I have had my tyres slashed, or a key scraped down my paint work,' Monteith said anxiously.

'Tenner to look after your car, mister,' a kid shouted from across the road. 'I'll do it for a fiver,' another one chipped in, then burst out laughing.

The hostel was a three-storey building dating back to when Thelwell was first built. It started out as fancy flats, but over the years owners moved out and squatters moved in. Now refurbished by the council, it had an electronic buzzer system which you had to push before being allowed in. Watson pushed the button marked "office". There was a CCTV camera on the wall above the door. They waited about twenty seconds before a female voice answered.

'Yes, who is it?'

'DCI Watson and DS Monteith, from the Ravenswood police, madam.'

'Show your IDs to the CCTV please.'

They both took out their IDs and held them up. The door buzzed and unlocked, and they stepped through into a large hall.

'Hello, I'm Sheila Evans, the manager here.' A tall thin lady, dressed in dungarees, a yellow t-shirt and a bandana, came forward and shook their hands. Sheila directed them into her small office. The room was a tight squeeze, with apart from a large desk, two guest chairs and two tall filing cabinets. She sat behind her desk, covered in paperwork and a computer. Watson looked around before sitting in one of the two guest chairs.

'What can I help you with?' Sheila asked.

'Ronald Freeman. His driver's licence gave this as his address,' Watson said.

'Yes, he's been living here for about three months. It's very shocking, his death.' Sheila's voice trembled. 'His sister rang this morning. Do you know who it was yet?'

'No, it's too early in the investigation. That's why we're here. What did you say? His sister Elizabeth rang this morning?'

'Yes, she is a regular visitor here, or should I say was. Visited Ronald about three times a week. Making sure he was ok for food and other things. He moved in here just after he came out of prison. His sister arranged the accommodation for him. Tried to get him back into mainstream life. She helped him to look for a job by accompanying him to the Job Centre and helped him claim benefits. She paid his rent as well. He spends, sorry spent, some evenings at her pub. Elizabeth mentioned moving him into a flat nearer to where she lived.'

Sheila stared out of the window at the kids outside and then back at the detectives. 'You can't blame her for wanting him to live closer to her. You know what this area is like.'

'Did he have any other visitors?'

'No... not that I know of. But I heard him say a couple of times over the last week or so that he thought he was being followed. Elizabeth put it down to paranoia. Being cooped up in prison all that time watching your back and then released into society. I suppose you are bound to feel... well vulnerable, shall we say.'

'Did he give you or his sister a description of the person he thought was following him?'

'No, but you know what this area is like. Kids and other people hanging around the streets, looking after number one, or whoever pays them as lookouts. He might have mistaken one of them. If there was a stranger around this area, then word soon gets out. The local grapevine stretches a long way and is quick. You being here would have gone around the estate by now.'

'Any chance we can we look in his room?' Watson asked.

'I'm afraid I cannot allow that. Not unless you have a warrant, and his sister is present. She has asked for nobody to go in for now.' Sheila replied.

There was a knock on the office door. 'Yes?' Sheila said.

A young man stuck his head round the door. 'Sorry, didn't know you had company. Sheila, a bulb has blown on the second-floor landing.'

'Ok Mike, I will be there soon, thank you. Chief Inspector, Sergeant, I'm sorry to cut this short, but it looks like I am wanted. No rest for the workers. I will see you out.'

There were still kids and teenagers hanging around across the street by the shop. Monteith quickly went over to his car to check it still had four wheels, and the paint was intact.

'Do you get a lot of trouble with the kids round here?' Watson asked Sheila, as Monteith was frantically looking for his keys.

'Funnily enough, no. They know what happens in this area stays in this area, and you do nothing to your neighbour. They look after their own here, including us. Hope you catch the bastard that did this.' With that, Sheila disappeared inside.

CHAPTER THREE

Tired and pissed off because of a four-car pile-up on the dual carriageway, making their journey double as long, a grumpy Monteith dropped Watson back at his house.

It was a large four bedroom detached in Ravenswood's South Meadows area. Watson walked up his gravel driveway past his blue Ford Focus and his wife Sally's red Citroen Xsara Picasso. The Picasso was on its last legs, but they couldn't afford to replace it now. He noticed the front lawn needed cutting, and the borders needed weeding and tidying up. *A job for the weekend*, he thought, already feeling exhausted at the prospect of gardening on his day off.

What Watson needed right now was a hot shower, something to eat and, hopefully, a massage from Sally. He opened the front door to a wall of noise. *How four people can make that much noise I'll never work out*, he mused, locking the door behind him.

Rachael was in her pink elephant pyjamas in the lounge, singing along loudly to her music. The two oldest children, thirteen-year-old Simon and his two years younger brother, Jason, were arguing upstairs about something to do with a console game. Sally stood at the bottom of the stairs, her back to him, trying to regain order.

Watson took in her lovely figure, dressed in a tight red t-shirt, and a well-fitting pair of worn jeans. He smiled at the thought of that massage later and hoped Sally wouldn't be too tired.

The stairs doubled back on themselves. Coming off the hall was the lounge, which ran the full length of the house, walls covered in photographs of family and signed posters of his favourite rock bands. The hall continued through to a large kitchen with all mod cons and red shiny cabinets. Off the kitchen was a toilet and a wet room.

'Here's the cavalry,' Sally said, smiling at Terry.

'Nope, just The Lone Ranger. Tonto has left.' He pulled Sally into an embrace and kissed her hungrily.

'Daddy!' Rachael squealed as she spotted him and charged across the lounge and out into the hall. Terry reluctantly let go of his wife and picked his daughter up, swinging her around, with her long hair flying. Her laughter filled the house.

'I'm listening to my music. Here, listen.' She put her earphones on his head. Terry hadn't got the foggiest what he was listening to, but he bobbed his head, trying to sing along with the words, making Rachael giggle and Sally shake her head in amusement. Rachael took the headphones back off his head.

'I was enjoying that,' he said, faking upset, but with a big smile on his face.

'You're funny, Daddy.' Rachael was giggling.

'Right, young lady, I said you could stay up until Daddy came in,' Sally broke the revelry.

'Aww, he only just got in!' Rachael pouted.

'Go on up, angel. I'll come and say goodnight once you're ready for bed,' said Terry, herding her toward the stairs and clapping his hands, chuckling at her expression as she stomped upstairs.

'Food or shower first, Mr Lone Ranger?' Sally said as Terry wrapped her in his arms from behind.

'Food first. I might need help in the shower later.'

'Oh, really?' Sally turned around with an impish grin on her face.

On the other side of the city, Jackson Davis stopped his black Toyota in Austin Lane, part of the red-light district.

Winding down the passenger window, he beckoned a small red-head who was standing on her own next to a high wall. She was barely over five foot, even on red shiny high heels, and wore a small shiny sequined red crop top and a black leather-look mini skirt.

'Fancy a good night?' she said in a husky voice, playing with her hair.

Davis smiled. He patted the passenger seat, 'Get in and I'll give you the best night of your life.'

Before she could open the door, suddenly she was thrown on the ground. Her attacker shoved her out of the way and piled into the back seat of Davis' car. He pulled out a Glock and pointed it at Davis.

'DRIVE NOW IF YOU KNOW WHAT'S GOOD FOR YOU,' he bellowed.

Davis froze.

'DRIVE!' Littlewood shouted, hitting the back of the driver's seat.

Davis shoved his car in gear and spun it away from the curb. The small redhead was sprawled out on the pavement.

'Drive where?' he said hoarsely. Littlewood caught him glancing in the rear-view mirror.

'Look ahead,' he barked. 'Go to the Barton Industrial Estate. And if you see a police car or try to signal to anyone, I will shoot you right here and now.'

'What do you want? Money? My car? You can have it all. All you have to do is say, I'll pull over and you can take it,' Davis pleaded, sweat on his face.

They drove out of the outer city centre on the main dual carriageway, and towards the Marsh Mills Trading Estate which housed Barton Industrial Estate.

Littlewood's voice sounded detached as he waved his gun around. 'Jackson Davis, former gym instructor. Jailed for torturing and killing two prostitutes twenty-five years ago. Released on licence. What would the authorities think if they knew you were bothering prostitutes again? Naughty, naughty.'

While they were driving, Littlewood reflected on the past few weeks he'd been watching Davis. That's how he knew the man was frequenting prostitutes again in Austin Lane, a relatively new red-light area with unsavoury landlords and seedy people. Before Davis arrived in Austin Lane, he had observed cars come and go, picking up and dropping off prostitutes. The desperate and the lonely looking for a way to satisfy their sexual urges, he figured.

He shook himself as Davis started to talk.

'You have me at a disadvantage. You know all about me, but I don't know you.' Davis looked confused and scared.

'Just shut up and drive,' Littlewood replied curtly.

As they came off the dual carriageway and entered the trading estate, they passed through a section of a well-lit road. Davis looked in the rear-view mirror. A smile passed across his face, ending in a huge grin.

'What are you laughing at?' Littlewood said, sitting forward, his hand gripping his gun tighter.

'Did you have a good time in the park today?'

'What are you on about?' Littlewood tried to remain calm, but felt flustered.

'Oh, come on Colin. That is your name, isn't it? Colin Littlewood? You were in the park earlier on, watching me. You thought I hadn't noticed you?' Davis spat. 'Or should I say former Prison Officer Colin Littlewood? Medically retired through stress and a breakdown following the murder of your wife Jackie. I believe you were on the night shift at Craythorn Prison. Two kids broke into your house, if I remember. Your wife disturbed them and... well...' Davis' voice trailed off.

'How the fuck do you know that?' It was Littlewood's turn to be surprised. He had a sinking feeling that everything was unravelling in front of him.

'I was in Craythorn when it happened. Surely you haven't forgotten that? It was all over the prison the next day.'

'Swing in through these gates on your right,' Littlewood cut him short as they had arrived at the industrial estate. He eased forward in his seat with his gun trained on Davis as he turned in.

The estate was a series of small boxy industrial units, four to a block. As they came through the gates, there were four units to their left and four others to their right, with parking bays for half a dozen cars in front of them. Each had roller doors as their main entrance for vehicles, and a small door which led to offices.

'Park over there.' Littlewood gestured with a wave of his gun to an industrial unit at the far end of one block. Davis parked up on one of the bays.

Davis looked shaken but continued. 'When those two kids Thomas Smith and Andrew McNulty were convicted, I heard they got a warm reception from everybody at Black Lodge Young Offenders. Prisoners and screws alike. And again, when they were old enough to be transferred to Claythorn.'

'Thank you for the update but our little chat has run its course.' Littlewood pulled the trigger and put a bullet into Davis' left thigh. Davis screamed in agony. Blood flowed out of the wound, soaking his trousers. 'You tortured those prostitutes, so that's what I will do to you before I'll put an end to your miserable life.'

'That's what *you* think.' Davis quickly put his foot hard down on the accelerator and aimed the car at the wall in front of them. The car lurched forward and picked up speed. Littlewood, surprised at Davis' actions, managed to fire one more shot at Davis. It hit him in his left arm. Davis' car smashed into the wall. All the airbags went off, leaving the inside of the car looking like a padded cell.

Groggy and bashed, Littlewood sat back up and took in the situation. Steam was rising from the front of the car; the radiator had split, and hot water was spilling out. Bricks from the wall were all over what was left of the bonnet and somewhere inside because the windscreen had shattered. Glass was all over the place. Davis was already half out of the embedded car, trying to make a run for it. But with a bullet in his left arm and thigh, he was struggling.

Littlewood, though dazed from the crash, opened the back door and slid out. Staggering around the back of the RAV 4, he saw Davis slumped in pain on the ground. He was clutching his thigh, crying out in pain as blood oozed out. Littlewood stood over Davis. Deliberately and like a farmer killing an injured animal, he fired two more shots into Davis' chest.

'Two down,' he muttered. He stumbled back to the entrance of the industrial estate towards a car parked with its engine running. He opened the door and slumped in, looking straight at the driver.

—

Susan turned her little white Renault Clio into the driveway at the front of their house. She turned the engine off, got out, and went round to open the passenger door. Putting an arm around her father's back and under his arm, she slowly helped him out of the car. He was groaning in pain.

Littlewood had needed his daughter's help in taking down Jackson Davis. It was Susan who had dropped off her father near to Austin Lane and had been waiting close by to make sure nothing went wrong. Her evening had been spent listening to the local radio station and humming away to songs she liked.

Then, when Davis' car left, she also left for the Barton Industrial Estate to pick up her father. When she arrived there, she'd watched her father taking revenge. For a moment, she'd thought everything went horribly wrong, but thank god, her father had got out alive.

Their next-door neighbour, Mrs Banks, was looking out of her bedroom window.

'Is your father alright, Susan?' she called out.

'Yes, he's just had a few too many tonight,' Susan replied, helping her father to the door while struggling to find her keys in her pocket.

'Do you need any help? I can get my husband to come down.'

'No Mrs Banks, thanks, I can manage.' With that, Susan got the front door open and eased her father into the house. She stood him up against the wall and locked the door.

'What did that fucking bitch want?' Littlewood shouted.

'Dad, that's enough,' Susan said firmly. She guided him down the hall, past the lounge and into the kitchen at the back of the house. Slowly, she eased his arms out of his coat and sat him down at the table.

'AARRGH my neck, my arm is killing me.'

'You have whiplash from the crash, and you must have bashed your arm against the door when you hit the wall,' Susan explained as she got a bowl of hot water ready and retrieved the medical box from the back of a kitchen cupboard.

'What the hell happened?' she asked, sitting down at the kitchen table.

'The bastard recognised me,' he said through gritted teeth. He slammed his hand on his good right arm onto the table. The few items on the table jumped with the ferocity.

'What? How?' Susan asked, staring at her father in bewilderment.

Littlewood spent the next half an hour telling her every detail of the conversation he had with Jackson Davis, in between the shouts of pain and curses as Susan tended to his wounds and strains. When she'd finished and dosed him up with painkillers, it was almost 1 a.m. Susan led her still shaken father through the hall and up the stairs to his bedroom, picking up his coat on the way up. She helped to undress him and made sure he was comfortable in bed.

'I want you to lie low for a few days, please, Dad. You need to gain your strength and recover from this,' Susan reproached. 'You've almost risked everything in taking down Jackson Davis, including your life. And I don't like it. It was stupid and careless. The police will be all over this. From now on, we need to be more careful about what we do and how we do it.'

Littlewood smiled. 'You're right,' he said, wincing in pain. The painkillers had not taken effect yet.

'I know I'm right,' Susan replied. 'Good night, Dad.' Susan kissed her father on his forehead and got up.

She went over to his coat on a nearby chair, removed the gun from the pocket and stared at it. Then, opening his wardrobe, she took out the rucksack, put the gun in it, and took out the red book. Opening it, she put a line through the name of Jackson Davis. She looked at the other names on the list, smiling as she returned the book to the rucksack and the wardrobe.

CHAPTER FOUR

Thursday Morning

WHEN WATSON AND MONTEITH arrived at the Barton Industrial Estate, they found about a hundred onlookers, gathered behind a section of crime tape. Mostly, they were workers from some of the industrial units who had turned up for a normal day's work, only to find a taped-off crime scene.

'Ladies and gentlemen, boys and girls,' Monteith burst out as they went past them. 'Here he is, the finest Detective Chief Inspector in the city, Terry Watson, and his humble servant. Detective Sergeant Monteith, that's me. Hhhuurrraayyy.' Monteith added a mock wave. Watson tried not to laugh, but failed miserably.

They surveyed the scene. What was left of the Toyota RAV4 was embedded in a wall. The rear left passenger door was open, as was the driver's door. Next to the driver's door, a white tent covered a body. Mac was busy buzzing around the tent and two forensics officers were taking pictures of the inside of the car. By another of the industrial units, uniformed officers were taking statements.

'Morning boys. What a lovely day,' said Mac cheerfully.

'I swear you love your job too much,' Monteith joked. 'Why are we here? Is it not just an abandoned crashed car?'

'Body under the tent has four bullet holes in him. My guess 9mm. Will find out when I get him back to the morgue.'

After they had put on protective shoe coverings and gloves, Mac held back the tent opening for them to enter. Jackson Davis was on his back. His eyes were open, full of horror. His chest was dark red with the blood from the two bullet holes. Blood had also pooled under his left side from the wounds to his leg and arm.

'Thanks Mac, we've seen enough,' Watson said as he followed the trail of blood which led from where Davis lay under the tent to the driver's door. He looked inside the car. Blood was all over the front seats and down by the gear stick. He couldn't see much because of the airbags, the broken windscreen, the bricks, and the crumpled dashboard.

Monteith joined him. 'Certainly no accident, but what happened first? The shots in the leg and arm, or the crash?'

Watson mused. 'The chest shots were definitely fired from outside the car. There's not enough room in the back of the car to do them.'

'Hopefully one of these units has working CCTV that will show something,' Monteith said, adding, 'I'll get one of the PCs to ask around.'

Watson turned to Mac. 'See you later in the morgue for your update.'.

Mac waved absently, focused on gathering evidence.

'Chief Inspector?' A PC called across. Watson turned, followed by Monteith. 'This is Mr Holland, owner of an engineering business. He found the car and body.'

Mr Holland was dressed in blue work overalls and steel toe-capped boots.

'I arrived about 7.30 this morning as normal. Coming through the gates, I spotted the crashed car. I first thought a joy rider had left it there. We get a few cars left here, some smashed up, and some burned out. It was not until I got closer, I saw the body.'

'Did you go near the car or touch anything before the police arrived?' Watson said.

'No,' Mr Holland said emphatically. 'Me and a couple of others went round as people arrived, telling them to keep back, not only because of the body but also because the unit could be unsafe.'

Watson nodded. 'Did you see anyone else in the area, hanging around either on foot or in a car you did not recognise?'

Mr Holland shook his head 'No. Only the regular cars owned by the workers here who come in around the same time as me.'

Before Watson had a chance to ask any more questions, a man in a suit and tie caused a commotion behind the crime scene tape. He burst through, walking purposely over to the crime scene. Two PCs were trying, and failing, to stop him.

'What the fuck is happening? Why we are being stopped from entering the estate and working?' He was shouting as he made his way across the tarmac.

'Excuse me, sir,' Watson held his hand up to stop the man coming towards them. 'Who are you?'

'It does not matter who I am. Why are we being stopped?'

'I heard you the first time, as did everyone around here,' Watson cut him off mid-sentence, obviously irritated. He pulled out his ID and showed the man. 'Again, I would like to know who you are?'

'The name is McGill, James McGill, if you really need to know. I own some businesses here, and you are stopping me from getting my deliveries out. Time is money, don't you know.'

He was a large chap. Watson had seen it all before. Men acting with bravado because of their size. The bigger they are, the harder they fall, he thought, before responding.

'Excuse me, Mr McGill. We have a crime scene here and until we have finished, I'm afraid that this estate will remain closed. Please, can you return to behind the tape?' Watson kept his voice level.

'What! For a crashed car which some little joy riding prick crashed? Haven't you got better things to do?' McGill was indignant with rage.

Watson lost his cool. 'Let me fucking show you if you want to,' he bellowed in McGill's face. He grabbed McGill by the scruff of the collar and dragged him around the car towards Jackson Davis' body.

'Hey what are you doing? Get the fuck off of me.' McGill stammered, trying to keep his feet. Watson flung back the flaps of the tent and shoved McGill in.

'Does this look like a joy riding prick to you? Well?'

Mac and his partner were sealing up the body bag to transport Davis' body back to the morgue. McGill could only see the top half of the body, but it was enough. He gasped at the sight in front of him. He gulped, ran out of the tent and threw up on the floor. After he had tidied himself up, Watson was waiting for him. Standing face to face, he lowered his voice.

'Piss off, or I will arrest you for obstruction of a police crime scene. Do you understand?'

McGill nodded nervously. He wandered off, muttering under his breath.

Mac appeared at Watson's shoulder, watching McGill trying to regain his composure in front of everyone. 'Interesting policing, chief inspector,' he commented, glancing down at the pile of vomit that McGill had left. 'Good job forensics have finished, or they would curse you for contaminating the area'.

Back in the car, Monteith had a smirk on his face. They were heading for the station, following the private ambulance which carried the body of Davis back to Mac's morgue.

'What?' Watson glanced at Monteith.

'I was wondering, guv, when did they teach us what you just did at police training, because I can't have been in the class that day. Either I was ill or in bed with that blonde called Carol.'

'Oh, piss off!' Watson replied. They burst out laughing.

'Wait, you and Carol?' he asked.

Monteith smirked again. 'Just a little homework with handcuffs.'

They both burst out laughing again but wiped the smiles off their face upon entering the police station.

'WATSON. GET IN HERE.'

The chief inspector almost jumped before he headed for the DSI's office.

Lorimer leaned back in his chair and smiled. 'Do you want to borrow my riot gear?'

Watson smiled back and gave him the finger.

As he hurried into Crompton's office, he noticed that Chief Superintendent Grant Matthews was there, his uniform as always immaculate, with creases so sharp they could cut glass. Not a single black hair was out of place and his shoes were shiny. Crompton, at his desk, looked pissed off.

The door was not even closed behind Watson when Matthews burst out. 'What the hell did you think you were doing?'

'Pardon?' Watson looked blank.

'You know exactly what I am on about. That stunt you pulled at the industrial estate. I have had an irate and angry James McGill on the phone. He said you assaulted him.'

'The jerk was interfering with the crime scene. He wouldn't get out of the way, and he was acting as if he owned the place,' Watson explained.

Matthews pointed a finger at Watson. 'That is no excuse. I had to calm him down, because he was going to press charges against you. I managed to talk him out of it. You are lucky he is not taking this further.'

Watson seemed gobsmacked. 'I'm lucky? He's lucky that he's not sitting in a cell downstairs.'

'Enough,' Matthews barked. 'Kenneth, either you get your chief inspector in order, or he will be back on beat duty before he knows it.' With that, Matthews grabbed his hat and threw open the door. He marched through the outer office, his face like thunder.

Before Watson could ask anything, Crompton put his hand up, got up from his desk, and closed the door.

'How the hell did Matthews get involved?' asked a stunned Watson.

Crompton sat back at his desk. 'Because it's not what you know, but who you know. McGill and Matthews know each other from the golf club.'

'What a surprise.' Watson flung his hands up in despair. 'But McGill behaved like a dickhead. We could have arrested him.'

'And he would have been out before you completed your paperwork. McGill may be a dickhead, but he is a dickhead with connections, and connections who control all of us.' Crompton sighed. 'But I must admit I wish I had been there to see what you did,' he grinned.

Both laughed.

'The look on McGill's face was priceless when he saw the body as Mac was zipping up the body bag,' Watson said, savouring the moment.

'Ok, so what do we know about what happened with this crashed car and the body?' Crompton asked as they moved back into the main office.

Lorimer brought them up to speed.

'Just to backtrack on Freeman, the door-to-door visits came up with nothing. And most of his cell mates are still in prison; those who have been released, have left the area. As for last night, the car, according to the DVLA, belongs to a Jackson Davis. The address is Manor Street. He's recently released from Craythorn Prison.'

'Another ex-prisoner. Two in two days, coincidence?' Monteith asked.

Everyone kept silent.

'What was he in for?' Crompton asked.

Lorimer said, 'They jailed him for the torture and killing of two prostitutes twenty-five years ago. Released on licence six months ago.'

'Okay,' said Watson, leaning back in his chair. 'We have two ex-prisoners, both jailed for murder. Both shot dead months after coming out. Strange coincidence? Or do we have a weird serial killer?'

'Apart from the fact they were both in jail, it seems a bit of a tentative link. How many get released each year from prison? Thousands? And because two get shot in two days, there's a nutter running loose? What do we do, stop them releasing prisoners?' Monteith said dismissively.

'No, but I think it's something we should consider,' Crompton cut in.

Monteith continued, 'Somebody must have held a grudge for a long time in that case, which is doubtful. Freeman was in for what… twelve years, Davis for twenty-five. No, I don't buy it.'

'Buying or not, let's concentrate on the things we can deal with,' Watson said. 'Lorimer, you take two officers and go to Davis' address. See if he has any family and talk to the neighbours. Keith, with me, let's see if Mac has started the autopsy yet.'

Monteith parked in the private bays around the back of the city hospital reserved for Mac's mortuary. The sign on the wall said Bereavement Care Centre. As they entered through a set of double doors and down into the clinical clean anteroom, both of them heard the blasting music coming from Mac's morgue before entering. They opened the frosted glass door to the sound of AC/DC's classic "Highway To Hell".

Mac was sitting at his desk, going through a pile of files, singing at the top of his voice. He looked up to see the pair of them head banging and playing air guitar.

'You two look like right pillocks,' he laughed, as he reached over and turned the music off. 'Bon Scott would turn in his grave.'

'That's loud enough to wake the dead!' Monteith came back with, shaking his head trying to regain his hearing. 'And who the hell is or was Bon Scott?'

'Ronald Belford "Bon" Scott was the original singer of AC/DC, who unfortunately took his own highway to hell back in 1980.' Mac enjoyed recounting rock 'n roll history to anyone who would listen.

'We have great sing-a-longs down here, me and my mates,' he said, going over to the freezer drawers. He opened one. 'Jane Doe here has got a wicked voice.'

'You're nuts, Mac. So, what are these two? Backing singers?' Watson pointed to the two covered bodies on the tables.

'No. These are fresh in today. Couple killed in a head on collision with a lorry. Driver fell asleep at the wheel. They didn't stand a chance. I was just going over the paperwork before examining them. Want to stay and watch?' Mac picked up a scalpel and a hacksaw from the table of instruments, looking at them longingly as if they were his pride and joy, which they were.

'No fear. You couldn't even pay me to watch you. It's bad enough looking at the bodies at a crime scene,' Monteith said adamantly as he backed away to the door.

Watson took over. 'Ok Mac, before Keith faints or does something else, we came down to see if you had anything on Jackson Davis. Have you examined him yet?'

'Nope. He is being prepped by my colleague, though, in the other room. As you can gather, we are rather busy at the moment. Would you gentlemen like to come through here so I can introduce you to the late Mr Davis?'

Mac opened the swinging doors to the adjacent room.

'I think I will wait here Mac; I can see perfectly well from here,' Monteith said as he came through the door and spotted the covered body on the aluminium table.

'Feeling squeamish, are we?' Mac chuckled.

'No. I will... well, stay here.'

'Ok Terry, you all right with this?'

Watson nodded, 'Yep, let's see him.'

Mac approached the table and pulled the sheet off Davis' naked body. 'Right, we have four bullet wounds. Looking at the ones on the upper leg, here, and the arm above the elbow, here, the angle of the wounds suggests the killer was sitting behind him on the backseat. The two in the chest were fired outside the car. Judging by the angle of them, the killer was standing above him and firing down. The broken ribs, cuts and bruises to the chest, legs and head came from the crash.'

'Are the bullets still in him?' Watson asked.

'No. I've already taken them out and given them to ballistics,' Mac said as he turned and picked up another scalpel. 'Sure you won't stay?' Hearing the doors fly open, Mac and Watson spun around, catching Monteith flying out through them.

'I think I'll pass. Looks like I've a sergeant to catch.'

———

DC Lorimer and two female constables arrived in a squad car at Davis' house on Manor Street, taking in the surrounding area. The park across the road was busy; the traffic on the road light. They walked up the drive towards the house, noticing the drawn curtains both upstairs and downstairs. As they approached, there was a movement behind the curtains downstairs. The head of an Alsatian poked through and started barking.

'Oh, what a lovely dog,' one constable said. 'My parents own an Alsatian called Buster.'

Lorimer looked at her. 'You say that now when it's safe outside. Let's see what you think when we get in there.' With that, he knocked hard on the front door. The Alsatian, still barking loudly, flew at the door.

'Is it still a lovely dog now?' Lorimer turned and smiled at the constable.

'Hello? Excuse me?' an old gentleman was walking up the driveway, waving. He was dressed in a shirt and cardigan with smart trousers and dark shoes.

Lorimer turned and took out his ID. 'Can I help you?'

'I'm sorry; my name is Donald Carter. I saw your car from my house next door. Are you after Jackson Davis?' the neighbour asked.

'Do you know Mr Davis well, sir?' Lorimer asked.

'Not personally. I spoke more to his parents. Very nice couple. Jackson keeps to himself. Weird man. When he was jailed for those murders, his parents never got over it. It was a big shock for them.'

'When did you last see Mr Davis?' Lorimer asked, pulling out his notebook.

'Let me see. I remember last night seeing his car here about 9.30 p.m. But when I looked out around 10 p.m. before I went to bed, it wasn't here.'

'Ok, thank you for that.' Lorimer jotted it down. 'There is no answer from the house. Have you seen his parents? We need to talk to them.'

'You will have a job doing that. His father died about four years ago. Cancer, very quick. His mother is in a home. Jackson had to put her there about three months ago for her own safety. Alzheimer's, poor woman doesn't know what day it is half the time. The wife and I looked after her after his father died, and before he came out.' Lorimer was scribbling, having trouble keeping up.

He turned to a constable. 'We will need a locksmith and a dog warden.' She nodded and disappeared towards the squad car to make the arrangements.

'Why are you doing that? I'm sure Mr Davis will be back later.' Mr Carter looked worried.

'I'm sorry to inform you, but Mr Davis was involved in an accident last night. I'm afraid he has died.'

'Oh God, oh no! How terrible!' Carter paled and looked shocked.

Lorimer beckoned the other constable over. 'Can you take him back to his house, and stay with him until he is ok, please?' She led the neighbour away, leaving Lorimer with his thoughts.

He had never been involved with a major murder enquiry before. Prior to this secondment, he was in charge of the outlying police stations dealing with delegating work, supervising investigations, monitoring law enforcement operations, supervising responses to critical incidents and managing resources.

Now building up to his detective sergeant's exam, this was his big chance to impress, and he was looking forward to doing just that.

CHAPTER FIVE

Saturday

A COUPLE OF DAYS had passed before Littlewood felt he was well enough to venture out.

Susan had been strict, allowing him to visit his wife's grave only. She was worried he'd try looking for the next person. In her eyes, he was definitely not fit enough for that. He knew she was right.

Littlewood picked up red roses up from the florist first. Jackie's favourites. They had grown them in both the front and back garden at their house. Jackie was always outside, tending to them, dead heading, spraying, and keeping the weeds down. Littlewood smiled sadly at the memory of his late wife. Parking his Skoda in the small car park outside the local council cemetery, he entered through the large gates, the red roses in his hand.

The sun was glowing. As it filtered through the leaves on the trees, it left a dappled look on the paths. There were a couple of other people visiting their deceased loved ones. A fresh grave was being dug in a far corner of the already overcrowded cemetery. Reaching Jackie's granite headstone, he knelt down and placed the roses against it. Tracing his hand over the inscription as he always did.

> Her Life a Beautiful Memory
> Her Absence a Silent Grief

After a mumbled prayer, he got up and sat on a nearby bench. His mind drifted back to when he first saw Jackie, at the local sixth-form college. Soon, they'd become inseparable, spending as much time together as they could. He remembered their first holidays together. Non-parent holidays. Nothing extravagant like jetting off to Ibiza or the Canary Islands but B & B holidays on the rain and sun-drenched coast of Britain, walking along cliff paths. Exploring off-beaten tracks, villages, and secluded beaches.

University had never been on the cards for either of them. They got jobs working for local firms, saving money for a deposit on their first flat. They were married soon after Jackie's 20th birthday. Eleven months later, Susan arrived.

Colin started working at Claythorn Prison, and they moved into the house they were to call home. The childhood sweethearts' happy marriage ended after twelve years one night, ten years ago. A wife, a mother, and his best friend, taken away in violence.

There could have been two people in that grave if they had not allowed Susan, ten at the time, to have a sleepover at a friend's. He had been on a night shift at Craythorn Prison.

The shift had been as uneventful as it could be until his boss called him into the wing office. An hour later, he was sitting at his wife's bedside in the hospital. She had sustained severe head injuries, a broken arm and two broken ribs, and was on life support.

His next-door neighbour, Mr Banks, who was giving his dog a late-night walk, had seen two teenagers running out of the back gate of his house, nearly knocking him over in their effort to get away. Mr Banks went inside through the open back door, and found Jackie unconscious at the bottom of the stairs, blood pouring from her head. He had called 999 straight away.

Judging by the mess the house had been in, the two teenagers were ransacking it when his wife had disturbed them. She had either been pushed or fallen down the stairs.

With the description Mr Banks gave, and the fingerprints t the scene, Thomas Smith and Andrew McNulty were arrested three days later. Charged with burglary and murder after Jackie had succumbed to her injuries. She'd never regained consciousness.

At the trial, both Smith and McNulty pleaded guilty only to burglary. A jury found them guilty of manslaughter. The pair received ten years.

Littlewood was driven into a deep depression by the grief and injustice. The Black Dog had hit him hard, he mused. And he wasn't proud of having sought solace in booze.

No wonder he lost it at work. He was ashamed to think of it. Hitting a prisoner, even if he'd goaded him over his wife's death. They'd medically discharged him soon after.

It was then he'd started to formulate his scheme for revenge.

Monday

Littlewood parked up at the end of a long tree-lined lane. Along one side were fourteen poplar trees, stretching so high it almost looked like they were touching the sky. Behind them, the fields were planted with various crops.

On the other side of the lane were large fancy houses and country retreats big enough to hold a party in and not disturb the neighbours. An estate agent's gold mine, Littlewood thought. *Just the commission for selling one of those houses would pay a year's rent.*

The lane was on the edge of a little village, five miles to the North of Ravenswood. It was a picture postcard view in the spring and summer, but a pain to get out of in the winter snowfalls.

Littlewood stared at the house at the very end of the lane. Number 10, also called Horizons. He had been here before with Jackie. But that was in better times. They used to be invited by the owner and his wife to the many parties they'd held. Team building, the owner used to call it. Drunken revelries would be a better description... Jackie knew it was soft drinks only for her if they were to get back home.

Littlewood alighted from his car and walked the few metres to the entrance of the driveway. Two brick pillars with large granite balls on top lead to a brick laid driveway which was large enough for five or six cars. Only one was parked there at the moment, a brand-new Mercedes C-Class. Well-kept holly hedges bordered the front garden. The house had a stunning mock Tudor-style frontage.

He knocked on the front door twice. No answer. Littlewood walked down the side of the house, with the detached double garage to his left. He could hear a lawn mower as he opened the side gate which led to the vast back garden. A swimming pool was in front of the patio doors. Beyond that, large shrubbery and trees surrounded an impressive lawn. On a sit-on lawnmower was the owner of this grand house, the person Littlewood came to see.

Retired prison governor Adrian Knowles reached the far end of the lawn, turned the lawnmower around and headed back towards the house. He looked up and noticed somebody standing on his patio.

Littlewood waved as he saw Knowles coming towards the house and turning off his lawnmower.

'Can I help you? How did you get in here?' Knowles frowned as he walked towards the intruder.

'It's me, sir. Colin, Colin Littlewood.'

'Colin? Oh yes, I remember, from Claythorn.' Knowles seemed to remember, but looked unsure. He held out his hand, 'How long has it been?'

Littlewood ignored the outstretched hand. 'Eight years since Claythorn. Ten years since Jackie.' His voice cracked. Even after all these years, talking about his late wife was hard.

'That long! I didn't realise it was so long ago. Since I retired from the service, one day rolls into another. How is your daughter? Susan, isn't it?'

'She has coped ok, though she's got her bad days. She's working now as an administration manager at a local firm.'

'Wow, you must be proud of her. And you? How are you doing? Are you working?'

Littlewood smiled inwardly. He saw Knowles relax and becoming more at ease. Exactly where he wanted him, he thought grimly.

'That's why I came to see you, sir. For help in getting back into the job market. I have had a couple of short-lived jobs since the service, but hoped you could help. Speak to your friends, or provide a personal reference?'

Knowles rubbed his chin. 'Erm, I don't know.'

Littlewood put his hand up. 'I can see you are busy. I was wrong to just turn up. I'm sorry,' Littlewood said as humbly as he could. He turned as if to walk away.

Knowles reached out and put a hand on Littlewood's shoulder. 'No... no don't go. Please come inside and we will talk and see what we can come up with. After what you went through, it's the least I can do.'

He led the way through the patio doors into the large living room. Two three-seater wine-coloured sofas dominated the room. They faced each other with a glass topped wooden coffee table between them. A landscape picture hung over an open fire. A 60-inch plasma TV hung on the opposite wall, with surround speakers. At the far end of the room, a large dining room table.

They went on into the kitchen, surprisingly small for such a big house. Knowles picked up the kettle.

'Tea or coffee?'

'Neither,' Littlewood replied forcefully.

Knowles swung round, kettle in hand.

Littlewood stood in the doorway, a gun pointing at his former boss.

'Colin? What is this? What are you doing?'

'Sit down now!' Littlewood shouted, pointing towards the kitchen table.

Knowles put the kettle down and slowly sat down on one of the wooden chairs. His eyes were flicking between the gun and Littlewood's face. 'Colin, whatever it is, I'm sure we can work something out.'

Littlewood approached the table. Hate was in his eyes. 'Too late for that. I needed help ten years ago, but got nothing. My wife was murdered, and I got no help.'

'No help?' Knowles shouted, 'We gave you a lot of help. As much time off as you needed. Close to six months, wasn't it? We arranged bereavement counselling.'

'COUNSELLING. Is that what you called it? It was crap, no help at all. The counsellor needed more help than I did.' Littlewood was raging now.

Knowles tried to take the tension out of the situation. 'We put you on shifts to help you look after Susan. Not putting you back on the wings so you could settle back into work. If I remember, you were in the prisoner reception area when you came back. You only had to work days and no weekends. We were all happy for you and Susan when McNulty and Smith got what they deserved.'

Littlewood screamed in Knowles' face. 'They murdered Jackie. They should have got more, but that sodding jury were conned by the so-called evidence.'

In a rage, Littlewood hit Knowles over the head with the gun. Twice. Blood poured down Knowles' face. Knowles rubbed the blood away from his eyes and nose as he tried to speak.

'But then you ruined everything, including your career, by turning up for work drunk, or missing your shifts altogether. And putting Freeman in the hospital with a broken nose was the final straw. I couldn't protect you after that.'

That day, he'd been sober enough to go to work. Sober, but in a foul mood, giving grief to anyone around him. There had been six newcomers that day. Stationed at his desk in the prisoner reception area, he watched serving prisoners processing six newcomers. Among the serving prisoners working that day was Ronald Freeman. As Freeman was giving out clothes to one newcomer, Littlewood had pushed him away, shouting to hurry up. Freeman replied with a sneer about Jackie and Littlewood had lost it. He managed to punch Freeman twice in the face before other officers restrained him. Freeman landed in hospital with a bust nose, and Littlewood ended up being sacked for gross misconduct.

Knowles, sensing that Littlewood was distracted, went to get out of his chair. 'Colin, please. Let's try to work something out. I can help you get what you need.'

'I don't need help from you,' Littlewood said calmly. He aimed the gun at Knowles and fired. Twice. Both shots hit the man's chest. Knowles staggered backwards and fell against the kitchen side. He slid down, blood pooling around his body.

Littlewood stood for a moment, watching. Then he turned and walked out of the kitchen, back into the living room. He looked out of the patio windows, checking if neighbours were looking over the hedges, alerted by the gunfire. All was quiet.

Quickly, he made his way back to his car through the side gate and down the driveway. Opening his car door, he slumped in the seat. He could not control his tears: all the pent-up emotion from the confrontation with Knowles came to an outburst. *Jackie, I'm doing this for you. I had to kill him.*

Susan arrived at her place of work, parking her Renault Clio in the employees car park.

The morning sun was so bright; she kept her sunglasses on while walking towards the main door. Talking animatedly amongst themselves, other staff was already present.

The main reception area was made purposely unwelcoming. The tiles on the floors and walls were a sober grey. The reception desk, always manned by two people, was behind security glass. CCTV cameras had been placed both inside and outside of the main door. No personal effects were allowed to be taken through into work areas. Employees had to put their belongings into lockers before entering.

Susan showed her ID to the reception staff and was buzzed through the sets of doors leading to her office. She walked along the carpeted corridor, called into the mail room, and picked up a pile of files. In her office, she put the files down on her desk and searched through them for two in particular. Once found, she opened her handbag and brought out two pieces of photocopied paper.

She inserted one in each file and then put the files back in with the others.

CHAPTER SIX

Trying to get three kids out of bed, washed, dressed and fed on a school day was akin to military action in the Watson home.

Simon and Jason were first, as they always left before the others. Simon was in year seven at South Meadows Academy. Jason was in the last year at the local primary. With both schools being next to each other, they walked together. Sally, a teacher at the primary school, took Rachael in with her.

As Watson polished off toast and coffee while watching BBC Breakfast News, his phone rang, breaking the tedium of wars, politics and so-called celebrities at glitzy parties. It was Monteith, and he was not happy.

'Can you pick me up today, guv? I have car problems.'

'Yes sure. What's up with your pride and joy?'

'You will see when you get here.' With that, Monteith had gone.

Watson looked at his phone, confused. He turned the television off and took his mug and plate into the kitchen.

'Who was on the phone?' Sally asked. She was getting Rachael ready by the front door, putting her coat on.

'Keith. He wants me to drive today. Says he has car problems but wouldn't say what.'

'He's probably only got it dirty and didn't want to be seen out in it. I swear he spends more time with that car than with Katie and the kids,' Sally said with disdain. 'We are off now. Come on Rachael.'

Rachael ran and wrapped her arms around her dad's legs, then skipped out through the front door with her bag strapped to her back.

'He's not that bad. I would be careful if I had a car like his.'

'There's careful and then there's neurotic. And he borders on being neurotic over that car,' Sally replied as she walked out of the door.

Watson pulled into Monteith's street and watched a recovery vehicle loaded Monteith's BMW onto the back of a recovery vehicle why he and his wife Katie were having a full-blown argument in the front garden. Their children, ten-year-old Rebecca and five-year-old Pixie, were looking out of the lounge window.

Watson jumped out of his car and raced over. He looked at the BMW. All of its tyres were slashed. 'What the hell happened?'

'Ask him!' Katie bellowed. 'He's fucked everything up.' She stormed into the house, slamming the front door behind her, ignoring the onlooking neighbours.

'What does she mean?' Watson asked in bewilderment.

'It's nothing,' Monteith was dismissive, and gave the neighbours a hard stare. 'What are you looking at?'

Watson tried to get Monteith to concentrate. 'Nothing? Katie's running around screaming at you. Your car has its tyres slashed, and you're saying it's nothing. What the hell has happened?'

Monteith walked past Watson. 'Let's get out of here. I need breakfast.'

Twenty minutes later, Monteith was tucking into a full English breakfast. They had driven in silence to the cafe near to their headquarters, much to Watson's frustration. He was used to his sergeant's moods, but this was different and, as much as a friend and as his boss, he needed to get to the bottom of it.

'So, are you going to tell me what happened back there?' Watson kept his voice low. The cafe was packed with customers. Some of the night-shift beat coppers were in there, winding down, going over what had happened during their shifts.

'The car is a warning,' Monteith said between mouthfuls.

Watson was confused. 'A warning? From whom?'

Monteith stopped eating. 'Jimmy Russell.'

'Russell? What have you done to anger that lunatic?' Watson tried to keep his own anger in check and his voice low as a waitress came by the table. 'Russell is not one to get on the wrong side of. You should know that.'

Monteith slurped his tea and then stared down into the cup, avoiding Watson's eyes. 'I owe him money, guv. Gambling debts.'

'How much do you owe?' Watson wasn't sure he wanted to hear the answer.

'Nothing much,' Monteith replied almost casually. 'Just five grand.'

'You owe one of the biggest crooks in Ravenswood, Jimmy Russell, five grand?' Watson exploded. 'You fucking idiot. Do you have a death wish?' He got up and stormed out of the cafe.

Monteith sat there in stunned silence, his fork halfway to his mouth. Other customers were looking over. Monteith put his fork down and wiped his mouth, composing himself. 'Have you not seen a domestic before?' he called out to no one in particular. He got up and walked out of the door.

Watson was sitting in his car, the engine running. His face contorted with anger. Monteith slowly got into the passenger seat.

'You need to get yourself sorted,' Watson said, staring straight ahead out of the windscreen. 'You almost fucked up your marriage before because of your gambling. And judging by Katie this morning, you are well on the way to doing it again.'

'She will be fine,' Monteith replied, shrugging his shoulders.

'FINE... FINE... It's a wonder she's not ripped your balls off. Listen to yourself. You have a family to look after now. Think about them for once.'

Watson pulled out into the traffic and headed for their headquarters. 'We are already looking for one raging psychopath. I don't want to go looking for another one in Russell because something has happened to you.'

At police headquarters, the atmosphere was tense. DSI Crompton was fuming.

'It's amazing how the press can link the two shootings together, when we've told them we haven't done so,' he said, throwing a paper down angrily. 'And Chief Superintendent Matthews was just here. He's not happy. Do you have anything to report, Watson? It would get Matthews off my back.'

Watson looked at Monteith before he said, cautiously, 'Sir, we have found nothing to link them. One was in a pub car park, and the other was at an industrial estate. Yes, both were shootings, but that's all. The newspapers love to hype a story up to sell more, but they know squat. They're just guessing.'

'Are we guessing? Have we got any leads?' Crompton pressed.

'We're looking into some things which have cropped up. But it takes time, as you well know. It's only been a few days and we've had no witnesses coming forward.'

Crompton grumbled. 'Anyone else with some news? It better be good.'

Lorimer began by filling everybody in on the visit to Jackson Davis' home, and the conversation with the neighbour Mr Carter. 'Now we know Davis went out between 9.30 p.m. and 10 p.m. on the night he died. We need to look at CCTV to see where he went and who he met.'

'Right, as you found out about Davis, you can have the lovely job of trawling through the CCTV images. We've already asked for the discs covering last Wednesday and they arrived over the weekend. They're all yours.' Watson smiled thinly.

'That's all right. I'm used to box-set marathons. I watched the whole of *Breaking Bad* the other weekend,' Lorimer laughed, getting out of his chair. 'Just remember to bring me lots of coffee.'

He reappeared three hours later, looking like the cat that got the cream. Watson called them into a side room which had a large screen so they could see the relevant pictures in greater detail.

'Where's the popcorn?' Monteith joked as they sat down.

'Shut up and concentrate,' Watson shot back. 'Karl, the floor is yours.'

'Thank you, guv.' Lorimer sat at the computer ready to put what he had found on the large screen. 'We know Davis left his house between 9.30 and 10 p.m. last Wednesday night. That information we got from the neighbour. It was difficult tracking his car at first because of its dark colour, but thanks to the licence plate recognition system, I have more information. These first few pictures show Davis' car travelling on the duel carriageway on the outskirts of the city between 10.40 p.m. and 11 p.m. We see Davis then taking the junction off, leading to the Barton Industrial Estate. CCTV coverage is patchy on the estate, so there are no clear pictures we can use.'

Monteith's phone went off. 'Just going to take this,' he said, getting out of his chair.

'No, you're not. Sit down,' Watson barked. Monteith mumbled something as he sat back down, causing Watson to scowl at him.

Lorimer continued, 'The city centre pictures were hard to pick out with the volume of traffic and not knowing where he was heading. The first time we have him after leaving his house is on Crane Street, heading into Bankside at 10.05 p.m.' He put up the next picture. 'The next time we see him was close to Austin Lane at 10.20 p.m.'

'Austin Lane, interesting.' Crompton leaned forward.

'I lost him for a time around this area, but I picked him up, leaving and heading out of the city around 10.35 p.m.' Lorimer put up the next picture, a close-up of Davis' car. He continued, 'If you look closer, there is Davis, and there could be someone in the back of the car, but I can't be certain.' There was a black shape in the back, but it was unrecognisable.

'Thank you.' Watson walked to the screen, not taking his eyes off the last picture. 'As you well know, Austin Lane is the newest of the red-light areas which are blighting this city. It looks like Davis has started again to visit these areas.'

'You would have thought he would have kept his head down after being released. Six months later, and he's back at it,' Monteith commented.

Crompton shook his head. 'He's just sticking two fingers up at the justice system. You will not change people like Davis, and in all my time on the force, I have seen many like him.'

'If a pimp did him over, or a prostitute, that would be some kind of justice,' Monteith added, looking at his phone.

Watson noticed, but said nothing. He continued, 'Well, we need to find out what happened around Austin Lane. Who did he meet? Did anybody see him or his car? Anyone fancy some overtime tonight over at Austin Lane? We need to do this before it goes cold.'

Lorimer said he would. Monteith was looking at his phone until Lorimer nudged him.

'What? Yes I will.'

'Ok I will fill you in on the details later. Thanks.'

As everyone was leaving the room, Crompton looked at Watson, who nodded and called out, 'Keith, with me. Now!' He led the way to Crompton's office, shutting the door after Monteith entered.

'What the hell was that with your phone?' DSI Crompton was furious.

'I was waiting for a call,' Monteith explained.

'What? You think a personal call is more important that this investigation? More important to answer that call while we were going through information which could lead to a breakthrough?'

'Somebody slashed all the tyres on my car last night. The call was from the garage.'

'Whatever you have going on in your private life, you keep it separate from your work. Got it? Good. Get back out there. You ARE going to Austin Lane tonight, car tyres or no car tyres.'

Monteith stormed out of the office, leaving Watson and Crompton stupefied.

'I'd best check on him, boss,' Watson said, as he walked out in pursuit of Monteith.

In the corridor, Monteith was on his phone, arguing. 'Yes, yes, HOW MUCH? You are joking.'

When he noticed Watson, he mumbled into the phone, 'Ok, I will pick it up later.' He ended the call. 'Five hundred for four tyres, the robbing gits.'

'You had been warned, Keith. You cannot mix private life with work. I want you to get your head straight before we go back in there. Are we clear?'

Monteith nodded, avoiding his eyes.

Watson tried to calm Monteith down. 'I will drop you off to pick up your car and then let's get Austin Lane sorted. OK?'

'Yes, guv.'

When they came back into the office, things had developed. And not for the better.

'Right, gather around.' DSI Crompton brought the office to order. 'Change of plan. Just got a phone call. There has been another shooting over at Bennington this time. Watson, I want you to check that out. Mac and his team are already at the house. Here is the address. Lorimer, looks like I'm coming with you tonight to Austin Lane. Let's get going.'

It was almost evening when Monteith and Watson got to Bennington, each in their own car. They met up outside the house.

'Hope this doesn't take too long,' Monteith grumbled.

'Got some place to be? More important than this?' Watson threw him a look.

The driveway of the house was already taped off. Mac's morgue van and the SOCO vehicle were parked on it. The front door was covered with a forensic tent. After signing in, they took paper shoes and gloves out of the boxes next to the door and slipped them on. Inside, the forensic team was busy collecting evidence. Watson and Monteith went through into the main living room. They spotted a second tent over the patio doors. More of the forensic team were taking photographs of the patio area and dusting for fingerprints.

'Mac?' Watson called out.

'In the kitchen.'

They walked over to Mac and found him crouched over a body of a man, lying in a pool of blood. Nearby was an overturned chair.

'Evening detectives, we have to stop meeting like this,' Mac sighed. 'IC1 male. Shot twice in the chest. Also suffered a beating. See these two wounds on the top of his head? Not found the weapon yet. I need to take him back to the morgue and get him cleaned up so I can take a better look.'

'Was the attack in here or did it start elsewhere?' Watson asked.

'In here. There are no blood trails or splatters anywhere else in the house.'

'Do we have an ID?'

'The wife identified him. Adrian Knowles.'

'Where is she now?' Watson asked.

'I believe she is next door with a neighbour. Police liaison officer is with her.'

Monteith, who'd wandered off into the living room, called Watson. 'Guv, I think we may have a big problem.'

He was looking at some of the personal pictures dotted around the room. Adrian Knowles pictured shaking hands with former Home Office ministers and local dignitaries. The photos were from local and national meetings, some of which had national media coverage.

'Matthews is going to be in his element tomorrow when this hits the media,' Watson said as he inspected one picture. 'If this is linked to the other two murders, we are going to have trouble keeping it quiet. The media are going to have a field day.'

They left to go to the neighbour's and interview Mrs Knowles. She confirmed that she and her neighbour had been shopping in the morning. Her husband had told her he was going to work in the garden. When she came back around two o'clock, she found his body in the kitchen.

No, they were not expecting visitors and no, there had been no threats against her husband.

As they were leaving the house, they noticed a growing presence of the media. Uniforms were keeping them well back behind the tape at the end of the road. Even so, they were taking photographs of anything that moved and trying to interview anyone they saw.

A constable approached DCI Watson at the bottom of the neighbour's driveway, introducing himself as PC Richard Parsons.

'I've spoken to all the neighbours along the road. Most were not at home this morning, but the owner of number two thought she saw something.' PC Parsons flicked through his notebook. 'She said she was looking out of the front bedroom window, when she saw a red car leaving the avenue at high speed around 11 a.m.'

'Did she recognise the car?' Watson asked.

'No. She said with it being a private road, she knew all the neighbours' cars. This was definitely an unknown one. And she didn't see the registration number.'

CHAPTER SEVEN

DSI Crompton and DC Lorimer, with two female PCs, were in Austin Lane to find witnesses who'd sighted either Davis or his car on the night he was murdered.

They split into pairs, Crompton and a PC covering one side of the lane, Lorimer and the other PC the opposite side. The PCs were in plain clothes tonight. If they turned up in uniform, the locals would be suspicious and the prostitutes would disappear into the shadows. Crompton had ordered the PCs to take the lead in questioning the prostitutes, showing them a CCTV picture of Davis' car. Crompton and Lorimer would observe in the background.

After the first hour, they still had nothing. There weren't many prostitutes on the street that night, and those that were, were less than talkative.

As they were taking a break, a woman's voice broke the silence.

'Little Kenny Crompton as I live and breathe. Looks like all of my Christmases and birthdays have arrived at once.'

Crompton turned round and came face to face with an elderly woman, dressed in a knee-length leather skirt, high boots and a tight-fitting leopard-skin top.

'My God, Angie McDonald, you're not still in this business? What is it, twenty-five years?' he exclaimed.

'Don't be cheeky, twenty tops.' She laughed, flicking her black, shoulder length hair back, showing her large golden earrings.

Crompton kissed her on both cheeks. Lorimer and the PCs looked stunned.

'Don't worry, I won't bite,' Angie laughed, tapping Lorimer on his cheek. 'I know your boss from since he was a copper on the beat. I owe him a favour. He got me out a few sticky situations.' Turning towards Crompton, she said, 'What brings you down here? In need of some company?'

'Jackson Davis.' Crompton watched Angie shiver at the mere mention of the name. He was aware she had known both the prostitutes killed by Davis.

'What's that bastard done now?' Angie said with distaste.

'He's dead. Murdered.'

Angie cheered, 'Good riddance.' Her smile disappeared when she clocked DSI Crompton's stern look.

'Trouble is, Angie, he was down here on the night he was murdered.' He showed her the CCTV picture of Davis' car. 'We came down to see if anyone remembers seeing it.'

'That's his car?' Angie asked, alarmed.

'Yes. Why?' Crompton looked concerned.

'I heard there was an incident with one of the younger girls, Cherry, the other night.'

A car pulled up across the road a few yards down from them. A young girl got out, giving the driver the finger and a lot of verbal abuse.

'That's Cherry,' Angie pointed to the girl. 'Looks like she had trouble with a punter. Do you need to speak to her now?'

Crompton nodded. 'Yes, I'm afraid so. If she has information, we will need to talk to her.'

Angie crossed over to speak to Cherry. After five minutes of what looked like a heated discussion, with lots of head shaking and arm waving, Angie beckoned them over.

Crompton showed Cherry the photo of Davis' car. 'Do you remember seeing this car around lately?'

Cherry nodded. 'Few nights ago. I was about to get in, but somebody shoved me out of the way.'

'Do you remember what the person who shoved you looked like?'

She shook her head. 'He shoved me onto the ground, but I heard a lot of shouting from the car.'

'Shouting? Inside the car?' Crompton exchanged looks with Lorimer. 'Can you remember what they said, Cherry?'

'It was something like "DRIVE NOW", and "WHAT'S GOOD FOR YOU". The next thing the car door shut, and it took off, spraying me with muck.' She showed them the cuts and grazes on her legs.

'Thank you, Cherry. We need you to come in and make a statement,' DS Lorimer said.

Cherry rocked her head and backed off. Angie touched her arm lightly, trying to calm her down. They stepped away and spoke in hushed voices.

'I'll bring her down tomorrow for a statement,' Angie said, coming back to them. 'She is young and naive. She's also had a hard upbringing. Drugged up and drunk parents. Will the afternoon be alright?'

'Yes, thanks, Angie.' Crompton kissed her on the cheek again. 'Don't make it so long next time,' Angie whispered in his ear. The PCs smirked as they saw their boss blush.

Susan walked into the house after another tough day at work. She was exhausted. Working there was hard, and definitely not a place she would have chosen, but needs must. Her world had turned upside down when she was ten. The murder of her mother. Her father falling apart. She had had to grow up fast, looking after him. No chance of a carefree childhood like other children. Their next-door neighbours, Mr and Mrs Banks, had helped out. Mrs Banks tried to replace her mother, but of course, no one could.

As Susan entered the front room, she found her father slumped in his chair, snoring. An empty bottle of whisky was lying on the carpet. How long had he been drinking himself into oblivion? What happened? She knew she wouldn't get anything out of him now.

Susan took a shower, trying to wash all the foulness of her place of work off herself. Drying herself in front of the full-length mirror, she stood and looked at her naked body. At twenty years, she had curves in all the right places. *I should be out partying with friends, dating, and having fun. Here I am, stuck in a job I hate to help Dad. Family comes first.* That's what she'd done over the last ten years: support her father. It had been tough.

Because of that, she had missed doing all the things her school friends had done. Now they were going to university, taking a year out travelling, or getting married and having families. They had invited her to a couple of weddings, but she never went. Family comes first.

She had a boyfriend in the last year of school, Shaun. It only lasted a couple of months. Her father came first, and Shaun did not understand that.

She rubbed her body, looking at herself front and back. Cupping her small breasts, touching herself between her legs, wondering what it would feel like if a man did that. She sighed.

From downstairs came a noise of coughing and spluttering. Apparently, her father was awake. She pulled on a pair of tracksuit bottoms and a T-shirt, and ran downstairs to check on him. He was still slumped in the chair, staring out of glazed eyes, trying to focus on the surrounding room.

She left him getting his head right and went to start their evening meal. Putting on the DAB radio to the local station, she stopped dead when the news came on.

Reports are coming in of a shooting in the village of Bennington.
The name of the victim has not been released, but we believe he is a prominent local man.

Susan did not need to be told who it was. She already knew. It explained why her father was in his current state. She looked round to see him standing in the kitchen doorway. They made eye contact. No word was uttered. Susan went over and hugged her dad. Tonight was one for quiet reflection.

Watson arrived back home late that evening. The children were already in bed. Sally was busy at the kitchen table with school lesson planners, a glass of wine next to her. She looked up and smiled as he kissed her. He knew better than to disturb her and blasted his dinner in the microwave, took a can of John Smith's out of the fridge and retreated into his den.

After switching on his computer, he put Eric Clapton's *Slow Hand* CD in the stereo. Something relaxing to listen to after the day he'd had. He took a couple of mouthfuls of dinner and a long swig of beer before he checked the online local newspaper. They were already reporting on the shooting in Bennington.

Neighbours report that the man found dead in Bennington was Adrian Knowles, former governor of Claythorn Prison.

That hadn't taken long to get out, Watson thought before going through the sports headlines.

He googled Ronald Freeman. Pages of information popped up within seconds. Pictures, newspaper reports, other documents, including reports of the court case.

Looking at historical and famous murder cases had become very easy these days, Watson pondered. From Jack the Ripper to the Yorkshire Ripper, and from Fred and Rosemary West to Steve Wright, the Ipswich Prostitutes Killer.

Looking at the Ravenswood Telegraph website, he had to admit their lead reporter had done a superb job of recording everything from Fred Mason's murder to the police investigation and the arrest and sentencing of Ronald Freeman.

Watson took his time looking through the information. He felt his eyes get tired. *Better stop now.*

Sally wandered in, a glass of wine in her hand. 'Tough day?'

'Yes, the worst and it will not get any better soon.' He showed her the headlines.

Sally put her wine down and started massaging his shoulders. 'Just relax.'

'Relax when you're digging your fingers in that hard,' Watson smiled.

He took one of her hands and kissed it, swinging her around to face him. Moving her blouse up, he kissed her stomach. Sally played with his hair as his lips found her belly button.

"Lay Down Sally" came on the stereo. Sally stood back, laughing. 'Good timing.' She took off her blouse and skirt, showing her lace knickers.

'You want to see more? Come upstairs...' She sauntered out of the door to the stairs, giving Watson an eyeful of her pert bottom barely covered in lace.

Watson followed closely behind, leaving Eric to sing to himself.

Monteith pulled into his driveway. Getting out of the car, he noticed a car going slowly up the road. He stood as it drove closer.

'Nice set of new tyres you got there. Pity to waste them,' a man said, laughing. The car sped off, leaving Monteith cursing under his breath.

Katie opened the door in her dressing gown. 'Who was that?'

'Just some morons looking for trouble, no one to worry about.' Monteith moved past her, put his keys on the hall table and took off his jacket.

'After this morning, I'm scared.' Katie looked worried.

'No need, love.' Monteith took her head in his hands and kissed her on the forehead. 'I'm going for a shower.'

Monteith stood with the water flowing over him, shaking. He was scared, too. *How to get out of this mess?*

Tuesday

'Tell me what we've got before I go before the media of baying dogs out there.' Chief Super intendent Matthews was glancing out of the window, looking down at the ranks of TV cameras and reporters milling around.

DSI Crompton sat behind his desk, frustrated at having Matthews in his office. He had always hated the politics of it. Policing was catching the criminals. Whatever it takes. He updated Matthews with the visit to Austin Lane and Knowles' death. He couldn't care less whether it was enough for Matthews to feed the media downstairs. Not his job. He sighed before he got up to call everyone into his office.

'I have just shared our progress with Matthews so he can get mauled by the press out there. Off the records, we are certain to have a serial killer on the loose. That's not what we are telling the media out there, though they will draw that conclusion.'

Right now, we are exploring all avenues to catch the perpetrators of these heinous crimes.

The TV in the corner of his office was tuned into BBC News 24, and it was showing the statement live.

Crompton turned the sound down. 'So what have we got so far on these shootings?'

DCI Watson took his eyes off the TV. 'Ballistics said the same gun was used in both the Freeman and Davis shootings. A Glock 17, our issued firearm. How the hell did our killer get his hands on one? We've also a partial fingerprint from the back of Davis' car, but too small for a match from the database.'

'We have one prostitute from Austin Lane, who had a lucky escape, coming in this afternoon to make a statement,' Crompton added, lowering himself in his seat again.

'I hear you bumped into an old girlfriend last night, boss?' Watson said with a mischievous smile.

'If you are looking for me to bite back at that comment...' Crompton stared back at him. 'We believe now that Davis' assailant got into his car in Austin Lane and ordered him to drive away from there. Judging from the CCTV pictures Lorimer showed us yesterday, they went directly to the industrial estate. Hopefully, we can get a better description of them later today.'

Crompton's mobile phone buzzed away on his desk. He picked it up, looked at it and diverted the call. 'What about Knowles?' he continued.

'Mac is doing the autopsy today,' Watson continued. 'Knowles was shot, but he was also hit over the head. Could be possible that whoever we are looking for is losing it? The first two killings were clinical, but this one was, I may be wrong, personal?'

On the screen, Matthews had finished his media mauling, and the reporter was summing up.

'So, who are we looking for?' Crompton asked. 'A former prisoner with a huge grudge?'

'How many prisoners get released from Claythorn daily?' Monteith asked. 'That's many people to track down and interview.'

'Maybe we can cut that down,' Watson suggested. 'When were Freeman and Davis released from Claythorn, Lorimer?'

'Can't remember but I will look now.' Lorimer was already halfway out of Crompton's office.

Crompton's phone rang again. He picked it up, pressed a few keys, and put it into his pocket. Getting up from his chair, he said, 'I'll leave this in your hands now, Watson. I have a meeting I need to be at.' He picked up his coat and strode out of the office.

Monteith nudged Watson. 'What do you make of that? Is he going to see that bird down at Austin Lane perhaps?'

'I am positive there is something he is not telling us.' Watson sounded puzzled.

'Are you still on about that, guv?'

Watson shook his head, then said, 'Karl, have you found out about Davis and Freeman's release dates?'

'Both were released in the last six months, Freeman first.'

'When did Knowles retire as governor?' Watson asked.

'If I remember, one of those photos we saw at his house was from a retirement party. I think it was dated about four months ago,' Monteith recollected.

'I can just about get my head around somebody taking out Freeman and Davis, but the ex-governor of the prison? Seriously?' Lorimer quizzed. 'Whoever did that must have known it would attract lots of media attention and become high profile.'

Watson perched on the edge of a desk. 'It depends on the killer's state of mind. If he is determined, it does not matter what we do. We could be dealing with a psychopath.'

'How did the killer know when Freeman and Davis were released? Knowles is easy; they plastered his picture all over the local papers announcing his retirement, and the new governor coming in.'

'Good thinking,' Watson nodded. 'We need to ask Claythorn for a list of inmates released at the same time. Karl, can you ring Claythorn and see if we can get that information? Be interesting to see what comes back.'

'I'll do it now.'

DSI Crompton parked his car in front of the Dragon's Den. This was one visit he did not want to make, but he had to. He knew the reception he'd get if he would be allowed in, that is.

He tightened up his tie and strode into the pub, going straight towards the lounge side of the pub. The landlord, Peter Preston, was serving behind the bar. Crompton ordered a half of bitter then asked, 'Is Elizabeth around?'

'She is upstairs. Who's after her?'

Crompton showed him his ID. 'It's regarding her brother.'

'Ok, I'll see if she will come down, but after this morning's press I doubt you will get the friendliest of conversation. And a warning: she has been drinking.'

Crompton paid for his drink and sat down in one of the easy armchairs. He took out his phone and flicked through his messages.

One from DCI Watson, asking when he would be back. He ignored it.

'Look what the cat dragged in,' Elizabeth said furiously as she came into the lounge, wineglass in hand.

'Hello to you too,' Crompton replied. 'You have a lovely way with words.' He waved his phone at Elizabeth. 'I had to look up some words you used.'

'Bastard.'

'Now I know the meaning of that one, and I am pretty sure I am not one of those. Can we go somewhere private?'

'Upstairs. The lunchtime crowd will be in soon,' Elizabeth barked.

She led Crompton through the kitchen and up a flight of stairs to the small private flat above the pub.

As they entered the front room, Elizabeth turned to Crompton, arms folded. 'What do you want, then?'

'It was you who called me, remember?'

'Oh yes, when were you going to tell me about this serial killer? I saw it on the TV this morning, just like that. No warning. Ronald's murder all out in public so everyone can...' her voice trailed.

'We only worked it out this morning. Chief Superintendent Matthew called the press conference. I had no say in the matter. I am sorry that you had to hear it that way, but I did not have the time to send anyone around beforehand.' Crompton tried to keep his voice level and calm.

'Bullshit. You never gave my family the time of day when Ronald was sent down. Why would you care now?'

Crompton huffed, 'Your father put pay to that. Because of Ronald's incarceration, he threatened me and stopped me from seeing you.'

'You could have stopped Ronald. I know you could've talked some sense into him. Robbing that stupid newsagent.'

Crompton didn't budge. 'Yes, if I wanted my brains blown out. And how the hell would I know what Ronald was up to? Besides, you know him. Once a plan, however stupid, was made, nothing would stop him. I was concerned and tried to speak to him but he just ignored me and said that if I would be in his way, both him and your father would pay me back big time. I'd only just been promoted to detective. I was intimidated!'

'I don't believe you. No, they wouldn't do that,' Elizabeth spat.

'Believe me, they did,' Crompton confirmed as he sat in an armchair opposite Elizabeth, who was again nursing a large wine glass. 'Listen, I didn't come over here to drag over the past. I came to update you on what's going on.'

'Your boss beat you to that,' Elizabeth said with disdain.

Crompton took a deep breath. 'Also came to see if you or your husband had recalled anything from that night or even the days before. Sheila, over at your brother's flat, mentioned he thought he was being followed.'

'He was always saying things that made little sense. We took it he was struggling to take things in after spending all that time in prison.' Elizabeth got up and refilled her glass.

'What things did he say?' Crompton stood up and gently put a hand on her arm. 'It might help with our investigation.'

Elizabeth took her time in answering, mulling things over. 'Yes, he did say that about being followed.' She added, 'Something about a red car hanging around.'

'Did he mention make or model?'

Elizabeth shook her head. 'No. After the years he spent in prison, the cars around now have changed a lot. I don't know half of them, never mind him.'

'Where was this? Did he say?'

'Outside the flat one time, then maybe when we were in town together. I don't remember.'

'When was this?' Crompton took out his notebook and wrote down the information.

'Not sure now. Sheila might remember better than me.' Elizabeth sank back into her chair, tears in her eyes.

Crompton knelt down beside her. 'We will catch who did this, I promise. What you have told me today is a good start and it will help. We now have something else to follow up on. I will see about sending someone to see Sheila again.'

'Thank you.' Elizabeth's voice was barely above a whisper.

CHAPTER EIGHT

A TAXI PULLED UP in the car park of the police headquarters. Out came Cherry and Angie. Where Cherry wore a blue tracksuit and white trainers, Angie had dressed as outrageously as the night before. A purple sequined top was squeezed over tight black leggings. A fake fur coat and sunglasses finished it off.

As they climbed the steps leading to the reception area door, two lads were coming out, chatting. As soon as they saw Angie, their jaws dropped. One of them held the door open.

Angie smiled. She gave them a quick look over as her eyes deliberately went down to the front of their jeans. 'Thank you, lads. I think you need to do something about them.' She handed over her card. 'Call me.' She blew them a kiss as she entered the reception.

Cherry giggled.

'If you've got it, flaunt it, dear,' said Angie, approaching the young officer at the desk. 'Angie McDonald here to see DSI Kenny Crompton.'

The officer looked up from his computer. He stammered, 'I'm... I'm sorry. Who... who did you say you wanted to see?'

'That's a terrible stutter you have there. You should get that looked at.' Angie laughed at the officer's embarrassment. 'DSI Crompton; just say Angie McDonald is here.'

'Right, ok.' The officer tried to regain his composure.

Angie, with a big smile plastered over her face, sat down with Cherry, who was chewing her nails, her legs tapping restlessly

The desk officer returned. 'DSI Crompton is out of the office at the moment, but DC Lorimer will be down shortly.'

'Thank you, darling,' Angie said.

'I don't want to do this.' Cherry suddenly got up and made for the front doors. Quick as a flash, Angie caught up with her.

'Don't worry. I will be in there with you.' Angie put an arm around Cherry and let her back to her seat. 'Listen, when I was your age, the man in that black car killed two of us. It scared us all. Some so much they did not want to help the police because they were worried that if the killer found out, they'd be next. A couple of us thought differently. We helped the police by keeping an eye out for him. And that's how he got caught. One girl he killed was my best friend. It's important for you to tell them what you saw, so we can get another killer off the streets.'

Cherry nodded and rested her head on Angie's shoulder.

———

Upstairs, Lorimer put the phone down after speaking to the desk officer. 'Angie McDonald, the woman the boss knew from last night, is downstairs with our witness. When is he back?'

'Don't know. He has not returned my call or text,' Watson replied. *What the hell is he up to?*

'Well, after your vivid description of her, Karl, I have to see her.' Monteith got up.

'Down, boy,' Watson stopped him. 'This is our DC's interview. Karl, bring them up here. You can do the interview in one of our offices. The ones downstairs might put off our witness. We need to keep her relaxed.'

'Relaxed!' Karl laughed. 'With Keith here behaving like a dog in heat.'

Ten minutes later, they were in one of the side offices off the main CID office. Cherry and Angie McDonald on one side of the table, Lorimer and PC Paula Dixon on the other. Drinks had been asked for and served.

Lorimer started. 'Thank you, Cherry, for coming forward. We value your help. The criminal justice system cannot work without witnesses. They are the most important element in bringing offenders to justice. We believe the information you have can help in finding the killer of the driver whose car you almost got into the other night. PC Dixon here will make notes of our conversation. You will then be able to read it over and make any changes that need to be made. First, I have to ask this. Are you willing to make a statement?'

Cherry looked at Angie, who nodded. 'Yes, I am.'

'I would like to take you back to last Wednesday night. Where were you and what were you there for?'

Cherry took a deep breath. 'I was on Austin Lane, working as a prostitute.'

'Can you tell us in your own words what happened that night?'

'I was standing waiting for another punter to turn up. A dark 4x4 pulled up next to me. The driver wound down the passenger window, and I went over to talk to him.'

Lorimer put several CCTV photographs of Davis' car on the table.

'Is this the car that pulled up next to you?'

Cherry picked the photos and studied them. 'Yes, this is the same car. I recognise the man driving it.'

'Are you sure?' Lorimer pressed. He *needed* to make sure.

'Yes, you never forget a face of a punter or the cars, especially the regular ones. Angie taught me that.'

'Was this man a regular? Had you seen the car before?'

Cherry hesitated. She looked at Angie before replying. 'Yes, he had been around a couple of times before.'

Lorimer glanced at PC Dixon. 'Have you got that?'

'Yes, sir.'

Brilliant.

'Now, Cherry, can you tell us what happened next?' Lorimer was enjoying his first major investigation. He had carried out interviews before, but only minor ones compared to this.

Cherry continued, 'As I said, the passenger window was down. I walked over and leant on the door. I said something like, "fancy a good night".'

'Did he say anything back?'

'It was... "Get in and you will have the best night of your life." You never forget a chat up line like that. Oh, and he patted the passenger seat.'

Creep, Lorimer thought. 'What happened next? Did you get in the car?'

'No, I was going to, but I didn't get the chance.' Cherry took a gulp of her drink and looked at Angie.

'You're doing really well.' Angie rubbed Cherry's arm, encouraging her to continue.

'I went to open the door, but I was pushed hard away from the car and fell to the ground. When I looked up, someone else was getting into the back of the car.'

Lorimer realised the next few questions and answers would be vital. He could feel his heart beating faster. 'Cherry, could you see who pushed you over before they got in the back of the car?'

'No, not from where I was. I just heard the shouting. It came from the one who got into the car. "Drive if you know what's good for you", that's what he said.' She added, 'He was banging on the back of the driver's seat shouting "drive". I scrambled up and moved back to the wall, safely out of the way but I could see into the car before they shut the door.'

'Could you see his face? Anything about his clothes?'

Cherry frowned, seemed deep in thought. 'There was not much light, but I did see brown or tan shoes, dark trousers and possibly a donkey jacket.'

'Right, I will leave you for a few minutes. You can go over what PC Dixon here has written and if you think of anything else, we can add that to the statement before you sign it.'

Lorimer left and headed straight to the coffee machine. His mind was in a whir.

'What's she said?' Monteith was keen to get all the details.

Lorimer walked over and updated DCI Watson.

'That's good news. We have at least confirmation of a few facts.' Watson went over to the information board.

Dixon stuck her head out of the door and called to Lorimer that Cherry and Angie were leaving.

'Right, Cherry, if you remember anything else, please get in touch. Here is my card. Thank you for coming in today.'

'Tell Kenny I am sorry I missed him,' Angie said she left the room. 'Bye boys,' she added toward Watson and Monteith.

'Bloody hell Karl, I hoped she behaved herself in there. Flaunting herself like that,' Monteith said when they were out of sight.

'She was the model of decorum,' Lorimer said, trying to sound posh. It sent them into hysterics.

'I trust you lot have got something of value to tell me, like we have caught the killer. Because if you haven't, why are we fooling around and not working?' Crompton had come in right at the end of the shenanigans.

'Sorry, boss.' Lorimer, still sniggering, quickly went over to the board and added Cherry's information.

'Karl has just interviewed Cherry,' Watson added, 'And you've missed your friend, Angie.'

'No, I haven't. She accosted me next to the lifts downstairs.' Crompton was still wiping the lipstick off his cheeks. 'What did Cherry give us?'

'A lot less than Angie gave you, boss.' Monteith's answer started another fit of laughter.

'Ok, ok, fun over. Point taken.' Crompton smiled as he walked over to the board. 'Fill me in, Watson.'

'The gun was the same one for the Freeman and Davis shootings, and we are pending the Knowles autopsy, so waiting for the gun used there. We have a witness giving us a partial identification of the killer from what she saw in Davis' car. And we have a possible sighting of an unknown red car driving away from Knowles' house.'

Crompton asked, 'That woman who looks after the building where Freeman was living — didn't she say Freeman told her he was being followed?'

'Yes, but Sheila Evans and his sister, Elizabeth Preston, put that down to paranoia. Freeman hadn't been out of prison long,' Watson reminded him.

'I know, but it might help to clarify it. We know from a neighbour that there was a red car speeding away from the lane Knowles' house is on. There might have been one at Freeman's flat? Watson, why don't you and Monteith see Sheila Evans again and check it out. Lorimer? Has the prison sent that list of released inmates through yet?'

Lorimer went over to his computer and searched his emails. 'It came in ten minutes ago. I'll make a start on it.'

Watson followed Crompton into his office. 'Boss, I tried to get hold of you when Angie turned up.'

'I know. I got your messages.' Crompton was looking straight at Watson.

'I thought you may have wanted to be here, that's all.'

'I had important business to take care of. Any problems I should know?'

'No, no. We will get off now.' Watson left the office, confused. *Did I just miss something there?*

DCI Watson was quiet. Monteith threw him a glance as he pulled out into traffic and headed towards Thelwell. He put the car stereo on to break the silence.

'Old MacDonald had a farm, ee i ee i oh,' Monteith started singing.

'What the hell are you listening to?' Watson finally said, staring out of the window.

'Oh, so you *are* alive... Just one of Pixie's CDs. Thought we would have some music on.' Monteith, straight-faced, burst into singing again. 'With a quack-quack here and a quack-quack there...'

Watson reached over and turned it off.

'Ok grumpy, what's up?'

'Don't know. I am convinced there is something Crompton is not telling us.'

'You still on about that, guv?' Monteith shook his head. 'If he has something to tell that we need to know, he will. Now we need to get more information on these killings.'

Just outside Thelwell, they heard sirens. Monteith looked in his mirror and spotted blue lights coming up from behind fast. They pulled over with the traffic and watched two Volvo squad cars and a Volvo dog handling car flash by.

'Looks like somebody called for taxis to take them into town,' Watson grinned.

Monteith burst out laughing.

A couple of minutes later, Monteith pulled up outside Freeman's flat. They noticed that there were no lookouts outside the shop across the road this time.

'They must have gone to see which house the squad cars have been called to,' Watson commented, getting out.

They walked up to the door, knocked, and showed their ID to the camera. Sheila opened the door and led them into her office. It was a bit more tidy, leaving them room to sit.

'What can I do for you today, gentlemen? I assume it's about Ronald Freeman?'

Watson started, 'When we were here before, you mentioned that Ronald said he was being followed. Can you help us with that? Did he say was it someone on foot or in a car?'

Sheila sat back. 'He mentioned nothing directly to me. It was something that Elizabeth commented on him saying.'

'How about the others that work here? Could he have said something to them?'

'It's possible. Do you want to talk to them?' Sheila picked up a radio. 'Mike, Steven, can you come to the office, please?' Both answered that they were on their way.

'Are you any closer to catching who did this?' Sheila asked. 'I saw on the news you are looking for a serial killer.'

'Investigations are ongoing but don't always believe what the media say,' Monteith said. His phone went off as he was speaking. He looked at the screen, shook his head, typed something and put it away.

Watson rolled his eyes.

A knock on the door announced the arrival of Mike and Steve. Their painting overalls were stained, it looked like they had more on themselves than what they were painting.

Watson started with the questions. 'Did either of you two speak to Ronald in the weeks leading up to his killing?'

Mike spoke first. 'Only in passing, really. He kept to himself. We took it to be a throwback from when he was in prison. He would say hello and mention if something needed checking in his flat, but nothing else.'

Steve added, 'Most of the time his sister Elizabeth was with him.'

'Did anything out of the ordinary happen?'

'Like what?'

'We are looking into the possibility he was being followed. He told his sister so. Did you see anybody or any cars around the front of here?' Monteith asked.

They looked at each other, and Mike finally spoke.

'One evening after having been at his sister's, he came in looking agitated. A bit worse for drinking as usual but he was upset. I asked him if he was all right and he took me outside. He pointed across the road as a car parked there moved off. He said it had followed him back from the pub.'

'Did you get a good look at it?'

'At a guess, a red saloon. It was dark and with only our security lights and the streetlights, it would be only a guess.'.

'Which way did it go?' Watson asked.

'Back towards town. I ran down to the roadside when it moved off, but it was too far down the road to see anything else.' Mike shrugged his shoulders. 'That's all I can remember.'

'Did you see it again after that?'

'No, we all kept an eye out for it, but I don't think it has been back.'

'Thanks for that lads, we will be in touch if we require anything else.' Watson wound up the discussion.

Later, as they were standing outside with Sheila, the police cars they'd seen earlier went past, back to the station. One kid who usually hung out outside the shop walked past.

'What's happened, Kevin?' Sheila asked.

He shrugged. 'The Claytons and the Edwards fighting again. I saw six of them get arrested.'

'Should be entertaining back at headquarters tonight,' Monteith exclaimed.

'Would not want to be the custody sergeant,' Watson agreed as they got back into the car.

———

The trip to headquarters was slow because of the rush hour traffic. Watson noticed Monteith was getting fidgety and stressed. Shouting at other drivers and sounding his horn a few times. At one round-about, a white van from a local courier company cut in front of them, causing Monteith to brake abruptly. He threw a volley of expletives through the open window at the driver.

'Calm down, Keith. Shouting won't get us there any faster, even though that driver is a moron for doing that,' Watson said, loosening his grip on his seat and door handle.

'I need to get back and away from work, that's all,' Monteith snarled, looking at his watch.

'Hey, easy tiger. You on a promise from Katie?'

'What? No. What you on about?' Monteith's answer was curt.

'Right, what the hell is wrong with you? What's getting at you so much you are like a bear with a sore head?'

'Nothing is wrong with me,' Monteith bit back. 'If you don't want me to drive, you can use your car. We always use *my* car.'

'Where the hell did that come from? Did I say anything about your driving or your car? I don't like your tone, DS Monteith.'

Monteith said nothing, pulled into the headquarters car park and parked up.

Watson said, in a more conciliatory tone, 'Keith, what it the matter?'

'Nothing's the matter. Get off my back, will you? Monteith jumped out and slammed his door, walking towards the back door without waiting.

Watson got out, flabbergasted.

Monteith locked the car and disappeared inside.

———

The custody suite sounded like a clash of feeding time at the zoo and a barroom brawl. The custody sergeant's face was red; he was clearly about to lose his temper. Nine officers were trying to keep order between the screaming men and women. Claytons and Edwards, Watson remembered.

He quickly went for the door to upstairs when he heard his name being called. 'Chief Inspector Watson, Chief Inspector Watson.'

It was Joseph Clayton, the head of the Clayton family, waving his walking cane about.

'Joe, what are you doing here?' Watson said, surprised. 'I thought there was a truce between you two?'

'Billy found out they were undercutting us on our merchandise and selling it on our part of the estate. He went over with his brother Davy to sort them out. I came down to smooth things over.'

And pigs might fly.

'Sorting it out? You mean they went over to teach them a lesson.'

'You are putting words in my mouth, chief inspector. Now that is not allowed.' Clayton wagged a finger at him.

'I've got work to do. Good to see you, Joe.' Watson turned to leave.

'Your sergeant seemed angry when he came in just now.'

'Case we're working on, nothing else.'

'Oh, ok. Pass on my regards,' Clayton said with a smile.

CHAPTER NINE

Wednesday Morning

Susan sat across the kitchen table from her father.

It had been two days since he killed Adrian Knowles and two days since he came out of his drunken stupor and massive hangover. Most of the past days he'd spent in bed or being sick in the bathroom.

Instead of leaving him on his own, as he might well have deserved, she thought, she did what she had to do. Family first... So she'd rung work, saying she had a migraine. She sighed. It'd been two years since her father had been on a drinking bender. Confronting and killing Knowles had sent him spiralling back.

Susan had searched and emptied the house of all alcohol so her father wouldn't be tempted again. She *had* to get control of her father.

She watched him tucking into a large fry up and a mug of tea. The first thing he had eaten in two days.

She would not pry into what happened at Knowles' house; her father would tell her in his own good time. Besides, the TV, radio and papers had been full of this murder. *And* the previous ones.

'That was good. It hit just the spot,' Littlewood said, putting down his knife and fork on the empty plate. He took a swig of tea. 'How bad was I?'

'Very. Don't you remember anything?' Susan asked, sipping her tea.

'Nothing, not since leaving Knowles' house.' Littlewood's face was a blank.

Susan filled him in on the missing two days. Her father looked shocked.

'I didn't realise what killing Knowles had taken out of me. The others... I couldn't give a damn but Knowles...' He shook his head, got up and came round to give his daughter a hug.

'Thank you for looking after me. I don't know where I would be without you.'

'You would already be in jail, or buried with mum.' Susan blurted, slapping him angrily on the arm.

'Fair point. You've got me there.' Littlewood put his arms up in mock surrender. He picked up the newspaper and read the front page. 'At least the police don't have anything on us yet.'

'*Yet* being the operative word,' Susan reminded him. 'Getting caught now by making stupid mistakes is something we should avoid, especially after all the hard work we have put in.'

She pulled the little red book out of her dressing gown pocket and smiled mischievously. 'Fancy doing a bit of a spying?'

'What do you have in mind?'

The smell of bacon and sausage baps wafted around the office along with that of strong, percolating coffee. The detectives were studying the list of recently released prisoners from Claythorn. All two hundred and fifty-three of them.

'Welcome to the biggest game of "Guess Who" we have ever played,' Monteith joked.

Nobody laughed.

'Guv, are we really sure that the killer is an ex-prisoner?' Monteith asked.

'No, but it's something we need to either confirm or pass over. We cannot do that without going through this list. Someone might stand out. What are you thinking?'

'Well, if you are doing this, with the ex-governor being murdered, do we include people working at the prison when he was there?'

DCI Watson mused. 'Good point. Someone who is disgruntled?'

Lorimer asked, 'Why prison workers?'

Watson explained, 'Because how does the killer know these people are ex-cons and are now out of prison? It has to be someone with knowledge of the prison system.'

'Obviously!' Monteith grunted. 'Duhuh.'

Watson ignored him. 'It could be an insider feeding information outside.'

'You and your theories,' said DSI Crompton, walking into the room. 'What proof have you got?'

'I just think we may be missing something if we just only concentrate on released prisoners.'

'Let's do this first and if no one jumps out, we will look at the workers, ok?'

Jimmy Russell was surveying his domain, standing on the balcony overlooking the casino floor. His casino. Situated on the outskirts of the city, it played host to the local wealthy and would-be millionaires spending all their hard-earned cash.

In *his* casino.

Born and raised on the Thelwell Estate, Jimmy's parents were one of the first to move in to the new council estate back in the 1970s. His entrepreneurial skills showed early at secondary school, where he was selling sweets in the playground, to the horror of the teachers. He got the cane. They found the snitch who grassed him up with a broken nose and a cut eye after an encounter with Jimmy and his brother Allan on the way home.

After leaving school at sixteen, Jimmy'd joined his father and Allan in the car trade. The second hand, ask-no-questions car trade. The "no one dares to complain or will find out how dangerous and vicious the Russels could be" one. Charming from the outside, ruthless inside. That was Jimmy. If people said he couldn't do anything, he found a way. His way or a hospital visit. He never married, but there were rumours of children he was supposed to have fathered.

He bought up failing local companies and turned them around in his own way, putting his own people in to run them. If a disgruntled employee did not like his ways, they would meet with serious injuries. Or worse... Nothing to be traced back to Jimmy Russell, of course.

He became friends with councillors and the powerbrokers of the city. His first few millions came easily.

Allan came over and stood beside him. 'Sometimes, Jimmy, even *you* outdo yourself. Getting the council to agree the planning permission for this was a stroke of genius.'

'It helps, dear brother, when you have something on the head of planning that he does not want to get out.' Jimmy smiled at his brother.

Susan brought the coffees to their little table in the coffeeshop. They were lucky to get a table near the front window as it was getting near to lunch time. Already it was filling up with shoppers. Mothers with baby buggies were blocking the way. Teenagers staring longingly into each other's eyes. Others were staring at their iPhones as if their world would end if they did not keep up with the latest gossip. Office workers were among the customers, holding meetings in there because the coffee was so much better than at their place of work.

Across the pedestrian precinct was a shop which was being fitted out. One fitter was Duncan Healey, released from Claythorn five months ago after serving two years of a four-year sentence for helping run a cannabis factory in a residential area.

'Interesting choice of subject,' Littlewood commented, smiling.

'I thought you would approve,' Susan, putting sugar in her cappuccino, smiled back at him.

'Are you sure *you* want to do it?' Littlewood asked.

'Yes, I think it would be best if I took the lead for this one.'

'But you have done your fair share already,' he protested. 'Is everything set with the other subjects?'

'Yes, the letters went out to the clients the other day. Nothing to worry about on that front.'

Littlewood looked across at the shop. 'Have you worked out how you are going to tackle him?'

'I thought we could work that out together,' Susan suggested.

Littlewood's face lit up. 'Sounds good to me.'

After two and a half hours, they had narrowed the list of released prisoners down to ten.

Monteith, looking exhausted, was pacing the office, trying to get his legs to work. 'Anyone of those ten stand out?'

'All of them, depending on what you are looking for,' Lorimer replied, 'Robbery, ABH, GBH, murder, extortion, drugs. This is a list to die for. Don't excuse the pun.'

'Any of them who looks good for our case?' Watson said, pouring another mug of coffee.

'Three of them are a good possibility, guv. Robby Davison eleven years for murder, Ian Smith four years for ABH, and Billy Clayton five years for GBH with intent.

Watson turned, 'Billy Clayton! He was in the cells here last night.' He pondered, 'They will be up at the court by now. I'll call in at his home later. But before that, better call in to see if Mac has done the autopsy on Adrian Knowles. Monteith, with me.' Turning towards Lorimer he continued, 'See what Davison has to say for himself.'

Watson and Monteith arrived at the morgue, where Mac's music was blaring as usual. This time it was Johnny Cash's "Folsom Prison Blues".

Mac was stripping off his scrubs. A sheet covered Knowles' body.

'Hello lads, come for your next instalment of autopsy for beginners?' Mac opened the bin and threw his scrubs in.

'No, just the findings please, Mac. I don't think Keith's stomach could stand it,' Watson chuckled as he approached the table.

'It's all right, I will stand back here,' Monteith was backing away to the other side of the room.

Watson commented, 'This is not your choice of music, is it, Mac?'

'I am playing it out of respect for our visitor,' Mac said as he pulled the top half of the sheet covering Knowles away. 'He was killed by two shots to the chest.' Mac pointed to the holes which were separated by the Y cut from the autopsy. 'But it's this which is interesting.' He showed Watson the deep cut to Knowles' head just above the hairline.

'Whoever did this was acting with force, lashed out in anger. Looking at the deep lacerations here and here, his attacker hit him twice. Found nothing at the house that could have been used for the attack. So perhaps the assailant took it with him.'

Watson looked closely at the wound. He frowned. 'Would the butt of a handgun cause that much damage?'

Mac nodded. 'Maybe? And from the angle of the wound, I would say you are looking for a left-handed attacker.'

Watson turned to speak to Monteith, but he was gone.

'Looks like Keith has done a runner again,' Mac exclaimed.

'Thank you, Mac. Can you email me the report when you've done? I think I have a sergeant to catch... Again!' He strode out of the mortuary, feeling frustrated with his DS. He stopped quickly, hearing Monteith speak.

'No, Mr Russell. I hear what you are saying. I will try but... Yes, eight o'clock tonight, I'll be there. Thank you, Mr Russell. Good-bye.'

Watson walked around the corner as Monteith was putting his phone away.

'There you are. What happened? You were there one minute, then you disappeared.'

Monteith twisted. 'It's nothing, guv. You know me and dead bodies in that place. Just feeling queasy.'

Watson patted him on the back. 'Just as long as you're all right. Let's see what Billy Clayton has to say for himself.'

The journey into the Thelwell estate was uneventful this time. At least Monteith put some suitable music on: Meatloaf's "Bat Out of Hell".

'Remember when we went to see him in concert?' Monteith turned the volume up.

'Yep, what an excellent night. Even with our other halves present,' Watson winked and laughed. 'We need to arrange a night out, just the four of us. Let our hair down. Old gits rule!'

'Don't say that last part in front of your Sally. She will ban you from the bedroom,' Monteith said, wagging a finger.

'Oh, and your Katie won't?'

'No, she will just ban me from the house,' Monteith laughed.

Both started singing along at the top of their voices.

As they got closer to the estate, Monteith turned the music down. 'You still think we are barking up the wrong tree, guv?'

'Yes, I have a gut feeling we are.'

'Is that the same gut feeling you have about DSI Crompton and the Freeman murder? Something he is not telling us?'

'Exactly the same. I think someone on the inside is feeding information out — when they're getting released, or have been released — and where to find them now.'

Monteith looked at Watson and shook his head. 'What are you suggesting? That they tell all the prisoners being released about a psycho hunting down ex-cons? I will tell you what will happen. Some of the hardened ones will say, "hold my cell" as they will be back for tea after killing the bastard.'

Watson shrugged his shoulders as Monteith continued his rant.

'And half the people on the Thelwell estate are ex-cons, or know someone who is. What do you want to do with them? Warn them? There will be vigilantes all over the estate gunning for trouble. It would make the feud between the Claytons and the Edwards look like a vicar's tea party.'

'That remains to be seen,' said Watson warily. 'Anyway, eyes on the road.'

They drove past the flats they had visited and the shop on the other side of the road, with the kids still outside. They followed the road around and turned off into one of the side streets. The Claytons' place was halfway down. A semi-detached house with a large front garden and driveway.

As Monteith pulled up outside the house, the curtains began twitching in neighbouring houses.

'Neighbourhood watch,' Watson said, nudging Monteith as they walked up to the door. Joseph Clayton had seen them and was already opening the door.

'Chief Inspector Watson, Sergeant Monteith. What a pleasant surprise. Please come in. We don't stand on ceremony here.' Joseph stood, leaning on his walking cane. His frail body underlined his years, but his mind was still sharp.

'You sit down, Joseph, I have the door.' Watson watched as the old man slowly walked back to his chair near the fireplace.

'I see the neighbourhood watch is alive and well,' Monteith said, as he was sitting down.

'Nosey buggers!' Joseph grumbled. 'Wish they would all bugger off.'

As they settled down, a red battered Vauxhall Vectra pulled up the drive. Watson and Monteith looked at each other. Two men got out and gestured towards Monteith's BMW.

'That will be Davy bringing Billy back from court,' Joseph said.

'You didn't go?' Watson asked.

'No. I've seen enough of the inside of the Magistrates to last a lifetime. We are on first-name terms with the judges down there.'

The front door opened, and both men strode into the living room. 'Who the fuck has parked their car outside our house?' Davy shouted.

'Boys, you remember DCI Watson and DS Monteith?' Joseph hissed.

Davy looked glum. 'Oh sorry, didn't see you there.'

'That's all right. We are here to talk to Billy,' Watson said calmly.

'What!' Billy exclaimed, looking like he would lose his temper. 'I've just been to court and you want to fit me up for something else? No way.'

'Billy.' Joseph's voice was stern. 'Shut up and sit down. Mr Watson wants to ask you some questions about when you were in Claythorn.'

'Why? That was years ago.' Billy sat on the arm of his father's chair. Davy plonked himself in the spare armchair.

'You have heard about the recent murders? The ex-cons? Well, you were in Claythorn at the same time as Freeman and Davis. Can you remember them?'

'You don't think I had anything to do with that!' Billy jumped up. 'I don't do guns. No. No way.'

'Calm down, we just want some information.' Monteith said, appeasingly.

'BILLY.' Joseph shouted. It was enough. Billy slowly sat back down.

'Billy, all we want to know is, did you run into them while you were inside? Did they cause any trouble back then?'

'Davis and Freeman? Davis not much, bit gobby. Spent more time in the gym than anywhere else. Freeman was on my wing. Kept himself away from trouble, except for one time.'

'What happened?' Watson asked.

'He turned up one afternoon with a broken nose all taped up. Would not say what happened.'

'There's fighting in prisons all the time. What made this stand out?'

'Yes, but those were prisoners who want to cause trouble. Wanted to be the ones with the authority on the wings. Or bored ones who took their frustration out by fighting. Didn't matter with who, other prisoners, screws, sorry, officers. Freeman was not like that. No, this was special because it was a prison officer who'd punched him. They say he didn't like what Freeman was saying.'

'Can you recall the officer's name?' Monteith was taking notes.

Billy shook his head. 'No, not now. It was so long ago.'

'Now Billy, you realise I have to ask this as routine. Where were you last Tuesday and Wednesday night?'

'He was with me.' Joseph jumped in, seeing Billy getting tense again. 'We were watching the European football on the TV.'

'Who was playing?' Monteith asked.

'Man United beat Copenhagen 3-0 on Tuesday, and Liverpool lost 3-2 against Inter Milan on Wednesday,' Billy answered.

Watson and Monteith exchanged knowing glances.

'Well, thank you for your help, and as always, if you remember anything else...'

Back in the car, Monteith turned to Watson as he starting the car. 'You believe him not being out? I don't.'

Watson shook his head. 'Not in a million years. He could have easily seen the scores on Sky Sport or the papers. He might not be our murderer, but he was doing something else those nights and not watching football.'

Back at the office, Watson filled in the others on what Billy Clayton had told them.

'Well, my trip so see Robby Davison wasn't so fruitful,' Lorimer said, 'Met his ex-wife. She said they split soon after he came out. He's now living somewhere in Spain, so we can cross him off our list.'

DSI Crompton sighed. 'Ok, there's nothing else we can do. Get off home and we will look at it again in the morning. Watson, see me in my office.'

He followed Crompton into his office.

'I have had word that Freeman's funeral is tomorrow. I want you and Monteith to monitor it. See if anyone turns up who takes an unnatural interest, or anyone we know and we have not thought of. You know the drill.'

'Yes, sir, I'll tell Monteith. He will be pleased,' Watson grinned, walking out of Crompton's office.

As expected, Monteith wasn't happy. 'Babysitting a funeral? Surely we have better things to do.'

'Don't piss me off, Keith. It's an order, and that's it. Now go home. I'll see you tomorrow,' said Watson.

Watson waited until Monteith had stormed out and then came back into DSI Crompton's office. 'Are you all right, boss?'

'What?' Crompton exclaimed, sounding frustrated. He continued, almost reluctantly, 'Yes. Yes, I'm ok.' He threw his pen on the desk and leaned back in his chair. 'Chief Superintendent Matthews is on my back wanting a quick resolution to this horror show, and I cannot make him see we are doing all we can. Without a breakthrough, we're buggered.'

Crompton looked washed out. His shoulders were sagging, as if he was carrying the weight of the world.

'We will get the bastard,' Watson tried to sound upbeat. 'We have things to track. He will make a mistake and we will be there when it happens.'

Crompton looked at Watson. 'I wish I had your optimism.'

'Oh and... Don't be too hard on Keith. He has things on his mind at the moment. I will keep an eye on him.'

Crompton did not seem to listen as his eyes were back on his paperwork. Watson left the office, closing the door slowly.

In the parking space, Monteith was waiting for Watson.

Without a word, Watson got in the car.

When Monteith dropped his DCI off at home, Watson noticed he didn't continue to his home but instead, turned the car around.

Why are you going back into town?

Quickly, Watson ran inside to retrieve his car keys. Sally was sitting on the couch, watching television. 'What's happening?'

'I'll fill you in later.'

'Grab a Chinese for us on the way back. Kids have eaten,' Sally shouted as he shut the front door.

He jumped into his car and tried to catch up with Monteith, hoping he could do so at the traffic lights. If not, he had a pretty good idea of where Monteith was going, he thought grimly.

Watson parked out of sight when he arrived at the casino. He was just in time to see Monteith go inside. He followed at a slow pace, walking nonchalantly but keeping his eyes peeled for his partner. The casino was not busy. People were playing on the fruit machines; some of the blackjack and poker tables had players on. Two of the high-paying machines paid out their jackpot. Screaming and cheering came from the players and those around them. He saw one of the lucky winners sitting on the floor in front of the machine, watching the money fall into the tray.

Watson sat at the bar and asked for a glass of lemonade, looking around for Monteith. After a few minutes, he spotted him on the balcony at the far end. He was walking along with a couple of security guards towards some large wooden doors through which they disappeared.

What the hell have you got yourself into?

At one end of the large office was Jimmy Russell, behind an ornate wooden desk. He looked sternly at his computer, tapping away at the keys. Monteith was shoved into a chair opposite him.

'Gentlemen, gentlemen, that's no way to treat our guest.' Russell turned away from the computer. 'Apologise please.'

The two bouncers mumbled their apologies and moved back, but stayed within touching distance.

'Sergeant Monteith, glad you could join us. Would you like a drink?' Russell was acting his imperious best.

'No thank you, I'm driving,' Monteith said nervously. He looked around the office, taking note of the position of the bouncers.

'Oh, don't leave me drinking alone.' Russell crossed to his drinks cabinet and poured a whisky and a glass of iced water. Putting the water in front of Monteith, Russell returned to his chair. 'I believe you have something for me?' Russell leaned forward.

Monteith fumbled in his jacket, pulled out a thick envelope and lobbed it onto the desk. 'There's a grand in there. Would've been five hundred more, but your goons slashed all four of my tyres.'

'Did they? Well, I am sorry if they got carried away. I will speak to them later.' Russell picked up the envelope and put it in his desk drawer.

'You're not going to count it?' Monteith asked.

'I trust you. Besides, if you've short-changed me, well, who knows what my boys could get up to.'

'Have you finished?' Monteith felt he needed to get out of there before his mouth got him into more trouble.

'Yes,' Russell lent back in his chair, 'I think that concludes our business for tonight. I will deduct the money from the interest payments. You still owe me five grand.'

'You bastard!' Monteith shot out of his chair towards Russell, but Russell's goons were faster, grabbing and holding him.

'Oh, by the way, on your way out, take your lapdog with you.' Russell turned his computer screen around. On it were CCTV pictures. One was a close-up of a man sitting at the bar. DCI Watson.

***

Watson was looking round the casino floor when the whirlwind that was Monteith hit.

'OUTSIDE. NOW!' Monteith growled.

The moment they stepped outside, Monteith swung round and landed a right-handed punch to Watson's face. Watson staggered and grabbed hold of his face. He winced and looked shocked.

'What the hell was that for?'

'Take your pick. Spying on me, letting Russell see you, not trusting me. Listening in on my phone calls.' Monteith was incandescent with rage.

'You're overstepping your boundaries, *sergeant*. I'm your superior officer,' Watson scolded. 'If you hadn't been so stupid to get mixed up with Russell... And you refused to let me help you. You're in trouble, clearly. Don't be a moron, let me help you.'

'It's none of your business!' Monteith stormed off, started his car and flew out of the car park, leaving a stunned Watson behind.

CHAPTER TEN

Thursday Morning

THE AIR WAS TENSE between Watson and Monteith. They'd each arrived in their own car at the council cemetery just before the Freeman cortege. Only official funeral cars and council vans were allowed into the cemetery. There were several cars already there, so it was a tight squeeze to get into the last places available.

They sorted out a good vantage point overlooking the area, not too close, but close enough. Neither of them wanted to talk.

Just along from where they stood, a middle-aged man was tending to a grave. They watched him clear the dead flowers and weeds away, putting fresh roses in their place. Kneeling down, he touched the headstone. It looked like he was saying something.

Freeman's cortege pulled in through the gates. A hearse with two official cars and three other cars followed. Slowly, they made their way through to the burial place, parking close by. Elizabeth and her husband got out of the first car, with other family members alighting from the other cars. Elizabeth looked around the cemetery.

Six pallbearers lifted Freeman's coffin from the hearse. The family followed close behind to the graveside.

'The amount of funerals I have seen over the years.' The man who was tending the grave nearby had moved next to Watson and Monteith. 'Some big and flamboyant, some small family-only ones.'

'And this one?' Watson glanced at the man before focusing back on the funeral.

'Normal size. Looks like close family and friends. I take it you're not family?'

'No.' Monteith showed his ID card.

'Ah. Whose funeral are you interested in?'

'Ronald Freeman,' Monteith said curtly, looking with frustration at the man who disturbed them.

'Oh, I read about him in the local paper. Nasty stuff. Is his murderer that serial killer you're after?'

'Investigations are still ongoing, sir. Now if you don't mind?' Monteith was getting pissed off.

'Hope you catch him soon.' With that, the man moved off towards the entrance.

'Stupid bugger,' Monteith mumbled.

Watson looked at him and shook his head.

'What?' Monteith smirked.

———

Littlewood smiled inwardly as he walked away from the two detectives. They stood out a mile. It was interesting to see the police detectives here, watching. What were they expecting to see or happen?

The killer turning up? *That only happens in films and TV series, right?* He chuckled.

When the man was out of earshot, Watson tried to get Monteith to talk about the previous evening. To no avail. Monteith was still grumpy and refused to acknowledge his trouble, let alone accept help. It reminded Watson of when Monteith went through the same gambling addiction. It had almost broken his marriage.

Then it had been the horses. Monteith could be found at the bookies when he was not on duty. And even when he was on duty, he made sure to stay in the knowledge of the day's results.

Katie had stood by him. They had only been married seven months, and she'd been pregnant with Rebecca. Monteith agreed to see Gamblers Anonymous and get counselling. It worked for a few years. But Watson could sense that this was much worse than back then. With Jimmy Russell on the scene, Monteith's gambling had exploded. You got involved with Jimmy Russell and nothing good came out of it.

How had he got involved with Russell? Why was Keith behaving like he was?

Watson could not just stand by. He needed to help his sergeant, his long-time friend.

Friday

For the last day and a half, everybody felt they were getting nowhere. Banging their heads against a brick wall. No new leads were coming in, but at least whoever this psycho was, thankfully, they had not killed again. Watson stared at the information they had collected on the board for what seemed the thousandth time. He could hear a phone ring. *What have we missed?*

Lorimer came and stood by him. 'Penny for them, guv?'

'You'd need a pound coin for what's in here,' Watson joked, tapping his head.

'Only a pound?'

'I'll give you the first few for free.' Both of them tried to crack a smile. Without success.

'The front desk has just rung. They have a Joseph Clayton wanting to speak to you.'

'Thanks, Karl.' Watson took the stairs down to the reception as the lifts were out of order again. That was three times in the last six months. At least he was getting exercise out of it. He did not even get through the door into reception before he was accosted.

'Mr Watson, Mr Watson.'

Clayton was there amidst a busy reception area. An elderly lady was reporting her bag being snatched. A man reporting a builder's van for dangerous driving. Two homeless people, well known to the police, were sheltering from the heavy rain.

Watson sat down next to Clayton. 'What brings you down here in this bad weather?'

The man looked around the reception. 'Before I say anything, can we go somewhere quieter?'

Watson agreed and went to look for a free interview room. He found one and led Joseph into it.

'I hope you will not tape this conversation, Mr Watson,' Clayton said, sitting down.

'Only if you have something you want to confess to, Joseph.' Both men laughed as Watson joined Clayton at the table.

'Now would I do a thing like that? No, first I would like to apologise for abruptly ending your visit the other day. It wasn't good manners on my part.'

Watson waved it off, 'Don't worry. It's all water under the bridge.'

Second, I asked Billy to really think about that altercation between Freeman and that prison officer, and try to remember his name. He said all he could remember was he had a name like Wood or Woods. They did not use first names unless you were chummy.'

'And it was definitely a prison officer that gave him the broken nose?'

'Billy said that was what he heard, but like we said before, rumours go around like wildfire. Only some end up being true.'

The rain was still coming down hard as Watson showed Joseph Clayton out before going back upstairs. He had asked the old man if he needed a lift home, but the offer had been turned down.

The reception was quiet; they had moved even the homeless people on. It was the smell, the duty officer told Watson. People were complaining.

Back in the deserted office, Watson added what old man Clayton had told him onto the board and stood back. With it being a Friday and information dried up, everybody had taken the chance to have an early start to the weekend. He had not noticed Crompton coming out of his office.

'You still here, Terry? I thought you had gone?'

'I could say the same thing to you, boss.'

'So what have we got?' Crompton came over to the board. 'We are looking for a man who wears a donkey jacket, dark trousers and brown or tan shoes. He drives a red car, is left-handed and is possibly called Wood or Woods.'

'He also knows about the prison system and can handle a gun,' Watson added.

'Come on, let's get out of here. We can't do anything else tonight.'

'Is Matthews still giving you grief?'

'Why do you think I want to get out of here? He's still in his office and I don't want to get called up there at this time on a Friday. He thinks we should be here 24/7.'

They walked down the stairs together and out into the car park at the back of the headquarters, saying goodnight to the staff on duty and dodging the early weekend drunks being brought in by two vans. The rain had eased, but it was still drizzling.

'Talking of grief, you and Keith are treading on eggshells around each other. Had a lovers' tiff?' Crompton asked as he got to his car.

'He's got a lot on his mind and I overstepped the mark the other day, thinking I could help. But I'm worried about him.'

'Could I do anything? Talk to him privately?'

'I will leave that to you as he's not in your good books over the phone and Freeman's funeral. Like I said, I tried and failed.'

Saturday

Watson hoped the weekend would be relaxing. Back to being a dad, he smiled.

Chasing a serial killer and trying to keep Monteith alive was more than one detective could handle. Three children and a wife was the better deal. Less dangerous, he thought.

Did he think less dangerous? Not when you are asleep in bed, on your back, and your six-year-old daughter takes a flying leap on the bed and clobbers you in the privates.

Saturday morning was football morning with Simon. He played in midfield for Ryland's under fourteens and the team was doing very well in the league. Watson volunteered to run the line. Not because he wanted to, or it was his turn, but because he did not want to listen to the bickering from the side-line over the serial killer.

Most of the parents knew what the other parents' jobs were. Though nobody questioned him about the cases he was working on, or that were mentioned in the local media, it was the rest of the spectators who were talking about it. Most were alright, apart from the theorists and police bashers. He did not want to get into a slanging match, putting them straight on the facts of the case. At least the linesman only got grief if he got an offside wrong. That he could handle with a big grin and some banter.

If his children kept him sane, his wife Sally kept him grounded. Fifteen years of marriage helped. Yes, they'd had had rough patches, all marriages do. He had seen the marriages of other police officers and detectives disintegrate before they realised things were wrong. Monteith's was almost one of those, but they'd managed to pull themselves back from the brink. But now... Watson hoped they'd be all right.

After the football was the gardening. Tidying up the flower beds and cutting the grass. Rachael was doing her best to help. Dressed in her red coat and red wellies, she was putting the weeds into her bucket and carrying them to the compost heap at the bottom of the garden. Both of them were dodging the flying football from Simon and Jason. Simon was teaching Jason some tricks and skills he had learnt during training.

It was different over at the Monteiths' home. Life at the moment was akin to a battlefield. He had not spoken to Katie for days, choosing to keep to himself, keeping thoughts of the mess he had got himself into in his head.

He usually got home late. Rebecca and Pixie were always asleep. Katie was sometimes up waiting, but most nights she was asleep as well. When she was up, it usually ended in an argument.

Monteith could not bring himself to tell her the full story of the deep cavernous hole he'd dug for himself. He knew he should. It affected the whole family. Each time he plucked up the courage, he'd sink away with shame and self-loathing.

Their savings had been depleted, meaning the holiday they had booked to Spain might as well be cancelled. He didn't even know if he'd be alive for that. Not if Jimmy Russell was after him.

How the hell am I going to get my hands on five grand? It would have been four grand but for that bastard Russell taking the grand I'd given as interest payment.

Sunday Morning

Duncan Healey was never one of the big men during his time in Claythorn. He was a minor cog in the gigantic machine that is the drugs industry. It was his attitude inside that had bugged not only prison officers, but also other prisoners. His only job had been to look after a cannabis factory in a rented house, and he could not even get that right. Caught red-handed after coming out of the house one evening completely stoned. In prison, he acted like Mr Big. Until they introduced him to the real Mr Big. Three weeks on the hospital ward followed, after they found him at the bottom of the wing stairs with a broken arm and leg.

Now working for a shop fitter, he was trying to turn his life around. He had even started jogging through the parks and around the lakes of Ravenswood. He had gone out early this morning on a route taking in the river; with only a few runners out this early, he felt as if he was on his own, just him and his music on his iPod. So it was a surprise when he approached the bridge over the weir and saw a jogger on the ground. She was holding her ankle and crying.

Duncan ran over, switched off his music, and knelt down. 'Can I help you?'

The runner sobbed, 'My ankle, I went over on it coming off the weir.'

'May I take a look?' Duncan smiled to put her at ease.

'Yes, but be careful.'

'My name's Duncan.' He straightened her leg so he could look at the ankle properly. 'I'm your knight in shining white armour,' he joked.

Susan smiled through her tears. 'Susan, and thank you for helping. I don't know what I would do if you hadn't come along.'

'Always for a damsel in distress... especially a pretty one,' he winked. 'Does this hurt?' He moved her foot slowly.

Susan winced. 'On the outside of the ankle.'

'There does not seem to be any swelling yet, but the sooner you get ice on it, the better. Do you think you can stand on it?'

'I will try. I parked my car on the other side of the weir.'

'You can't drive with that ankle!' Duncan helped Susan up, letting her put her arm over his shoulder for balance.

'I'm not going to. I will phone my father. He can come and pick me up.'

They walked back slowly over the weir. They were halfway across when he saw a man coming towards them.

'What are you doing with my daughter?' the man shouted.

Duncan looked shocked. He glanced towards the man and then back to Susan.

'Dad, what are you doing here?'

'I said, what are you doing with my daughter, you piece of shit?' He roared, dashing towards them.

'Dad, he is helping me. I hurt my ankle.'

'Shut up. I was talking to this piece of crap.' Littlewood pushed Duncan away from Susan and pulled out his gun.

'Whoa.... take it easy. I was only helping your daughter with her ankle. Tell him, Susan.' Duncan was up against the bridge edge with the gun at his chest.

Susan smiled widely. *That went well.* She'd played her part brilliantly. She waved at him. 'It's better now, Duncan, thank you.'

'What's this...?' Duncan was struggling. Fear crept in his eyes.

'Message for your drug friends, murderer,' Littlewood said acidly as he fired two bullets into Duncan's chest.

As life left his body, Duncan's eyes glazed over. His body slumped against the bridge end and fell to the ground.

Littlewood grabbed Duncan's arms, Susan took hold of his legs. They lifted the lifeless body and struggled to get it up, to throw over the bridge edge and into the river. It finally topped over and disappeared under the fast-flowing water sweeping under the weir.

Littlewood hugged Susan. 'How's your ankle?'

She kissed him on the cheek. 'Race you to the car and you will find out.' With that, she took off, leaving Littlewood laughing.

CHAPTER ELEVEN

Monday

CROMPTON ARRIVED EARLY INTO the office to have some time alone for his administration before the force that was Superintendent Grant Matthews would hit again. He cursed when he looked at his emails. All hundred-and-thirty-seven of them. Nine of them from Matthews wanting this and that. The deletion button was tempting this morning, especially before he'd had his first coffees.

One email caught his attention. It was from a newspaper titled,

Would you like to comment on this?

Attached to it was a Media Player clip. He clicked; it was a piece of CCTV security footage. Crompton looked closely. His anger rose as the clip played and he saw what was developing before him. By the end, his blood boiled. He emailed back, demanding to know the source of the clip.

Watson arrived just as Crompton had watched the clip for the third time, still trying to get his head around what he saw. He called Watson into his office. 'What the hell is this about? Why and how did the paper get hold of this? Do you have any idea how damaging this is for us? The force? The investigation?'

Watson looked nervous. 'I'm sorry, sir, but I think it's better you ask Monteith. I know he's my sergeant and my responsibility but he's also my friend. If he discovers I have been talking, you might find one of us in A&E.'

Crompton grumbled. 'Get Monteith in here, asap.' He turned his computer screen around when Watson came back with Monteith. Watson was clearly on edge. Monteith looked nonplussed.

'A newspaper reporter has sent me a CCTV clip from a couple of nights ago and has asked me to comment on it before it goes public. I wanted you to look at it before I do that.' With that, he pressed start.

The video showed CCTV of Monteith and Watson at the casino, inside and out. The last shot was of Monteith punching Watson.

Crompton sat back. 'What on earth am I going to comment? Do you realise this will go public? There's nothing I can do about it. I need an explanation, and fast,' he said grimly.

Watson froze. He could tell that Monteith was about to blow.

'No, it's none of your business,' Monteith shouted. He sprung up out of his chair, ready to storm out of the door.

'Detective Sergeant Monteith, if you set foot out of this office now, I will suspend you straight away, and Matthews will have to get involved. Now get back here and sit down. Whatever the problem, it will not go away if you behave like a spoilt brat who got his fingers caught in the till.'

Monteith hesitated. Watson could see the struggle on his face. Fight or flight. He hoped his friend would make the right choice. He watched Monteith slow down and turn around, back towards his seat. Watson sighed, relieved.

For the next hour, Monteith spilled everything out. That he'd started going to the casino about six months ago with some friends. A bit of fun, playing on the slot machines and Black Jack. That he'd come back and back and slowly lost control. That his friends first went along, but then stopped. It was only him. That was when he got involved with Jimmy Russell, who'd introduced him to the big league of poker in the casino's backrooms. It was only a matter of time before the high-stake poker games got the better of Monteith. By then, he owed Jimmy Russell five grand. The slashed tyres had been a warning.

Monteith added, 'That evening of the CCTV is when I paid off the first grand, but Russell said it was an interest payment. I still owed the scumbag the five grand. I was pissed off and seeing Watson had followed me, I exploded and hit him.' He looked drained.

'So we can take it Russell leaked the CCTV pictures to the paper,' Watson remarked. 'To show us he can do what he wants.'

Crompton had been silent all along. He was thinking, contemplating how to respond. He could, of course, suspend Monteith, but what good would that do? Lose a good detective in the middle of a major crime? He finally spoke. 'When does Russell want his five grand?'

Monteith sat slumped in his chair, looking beaten. 'You know Russell, he always wants things straight away or else.'

Crompton looked at Watson, 'I will have to tell Matthews about this, especially as the papers have got hold of it. You agree?'

Watson nodded grimly.

'I'm dead anyway. What's another knife in my back going to do?' uttered Monteith.

***

Lorimer was updating the information board when they appeared out of Crompton's office. He added three names, Gerrard Wood, Peter Woods, and Colin Littlewood.

'Just got off the phone to Claythorn,' Lorimer said. 'I was following up on what Mr Clayton had said about Freeman's altercation with the prison officer. They could not confirm that the incident took place because it's difficult to track down one from that long ago. But they gave me the names of three officers who were around then with Wood in their surname. All were working there when Freeman, Davis and Knowles were there. Claythorn are sending over what they have on record for all three.'

'This will not be another wild goose chase?' Monteith said, visibly shaken after the grilling he'd just taken.

'Sorry, but not all killers hand themselves in to police. Some we have to catch,' Watson said sarcastically.

'Ha bloody ha.' Monteith stormed out of the office.

Everyone stared after him.

'Who upset him?' Lorimer quizzed.

'Family troubles, nothing to worry about,' Watson answered. 'Right, when we get the info from Claythorn, we need to track down these three. Let's see what they have to say.'

Lorimer went back to his desk. 'That's just come in. It includes last known addresses.'

'I'll take Monteith to interview Colin Littlewood,' Watson said.

'Great. Lorimer and I will visit Peter Woods then,' Crompton said. 'Whoever finishes first gets Gerrard Wood as a bonus.'

—

Monteith was outside pacing around the car park, cursing to himself, when Watson came out of the door.

'I'm finished, you know that. Screwed. If he tells Matthews about this, I am out of here. You know what a straight down the line, by the book, officer he is.' Monteith slammed his fist down on the roof of his BMW. 'Bollocks.'

Watson tried to calm him down. 'They won't get rid of you. They need you too much.'

'Oh yes, says who? Lorimer is gunning for his promotion. Why not get rid of the embarrassment and promote Lorimer?'

'You forget I was also in that CCTV. They get rid of you, they will have to let me go as well.'

'No, they won't,' Monteith shouted.

Other police staff turned and looked their way.

'You will just go down to desk duty for the uniforms.'

'Why don't you listen to yourself? You're not the first officer to have a gambling problem and you will not be the last.'

'Yes, but I bet none of them owe money to the biggest lunatic in the city. If Matthews doesn't get me, Russell will. I cannot pay him off; like I said, I'M SCREWED.'

'We will sort that, promise. Now, come on, we have to visit one of the prison officers, Colin Littlewood. Let's see what he has to tell us.'

They took the long route to Littlewood's house so Monteith could calm down. The silence in the car was deafening.

After parking on the street, they walked up the drive past a white Renault Clio and knocked on Littlewood's front door. There was no answer. Watson knocked again while Monteith looked through the front window into the living room.

'They have gone on holiday.' The woman from next door was standing on her doorstep.

'Do you know where to?' Watson asked, as he approached her, showing his ID. Monteith followed with his ID out. The woman looked closely at them before she answered.

'Mrs Banks. And no, I don't know where they went. We came down for breakfast this morning and there was a note through the door from Colin saying they had gone away for a few days.'

'Do they often go away like this?' Monteith asked, putting his ID back in his pocket.

'No. I cannot remember the last time they went away for a holiday or even a weekend. Why do you want to know?'

'We were looking to talk to Mr Littlewood regarding our enquiries. Have you known the family long?'

'Ever since they moved here, twenty-odd years ago. Very nice family. Oh, here's my husband.'

Mr Banks walked up the drive towards them with his dog. Both Watson and Monteith showed their IDs again.

'Morning, officers,' Mr Banks said.

'They're asking about Colin.' Mrs Banks updated her husband on the conversation.

'Well, don't stand on the doorstep, come in.' Mr Banks ushered the detectives past his wife. She didn't look too happy.

They all went into the living room and sat down. Monteith and Watson on the sofa, Mr Banks in his chair, with Mrs Banks hovering around looking sour.

'So you want to know about Colin?' Mr Banks asked.

'Your wife said you have known him for about twenty years.' Monteith started.

'Yes. Colin and his wife Jackie moved in next door about then. Very nice couple. She was pregnant with their daughter Susan.'

'And when they moved in, where was he working? Did he have a job?'

'If I remember, he had just started working at Claythorn Prison.' Mr Bank's eyes narrowed. 'You cannot think he's involved in these killings, are you? No way, not Colin. He's not been in a fit state to do anything over the last few years. Not since his wife was murdered ten years ago.'

Watson and Monteith looked at each other in surprise.

'What happened to his wife?' Watson asked.

'You don't know? Two burglars pushed her down the stairs and she collapsed. He was at work when it happened. Jackie died in hospital. After that, Colin went to pieces. Depression, alcoholism, you name it. Lost his job at the prison. My wife looked after Susan because he couldn't. If you think he is a serial killer, you are wrong. He hardly goes out. The only time he does, it's with Susan, or to the cemetery to put flowers on Jackie's grave.'

Mr Banks was getting agitated. 'I tell you something. When he heard about that governor of the prison being murdered, he was so upset, Susan told me he drunk himself into a stupor. Is that someone who could murder someone? Tell me!'

Mrs Banks put a hand on her husband's shoulder. He started coughing terribly. She hastily picked up his Ventolin and gave it to him.

Watson and Monteith stayed silent, letting Mr Banks regain his breath.

'Mr Banks, are you ok to continue? We only have one more question to ask,' Monteith said.

Mr Banks nodded.

'You said he lost his job at the prison after his wife died. Do you remember why?'

Mr Banks leant back in his chair, bolstered by cushions. 'Something about a prisoner goading him over losing Jackie. Colin snapped and hit him. That was enough for the prison to get rid of him. It was the last straw on top of the alcohol issues. He could barely look after himself, let alone his daughter. That's why we basically brought up Susan. Helped her with her homework, took her in to sleep many times. Saw her turn from a girl to a young woman. Social Services got involved but because we were looking after her, she didn't have to go into care, thank God. Losing Susan would have just finished him.'

They thanked the Banks for their help, and Mrs Banks showed them to the door.

Monteith quickly asked, 'Mrs Banks, just to confirm, Mrs Littlewood's grave is at the cemetery?'

'Yes. Why?'

'Oh nothing, I can't remember if I made a note of it when your husband was talking. Thank you.'

Walking back to the car, Watson said what they were both thinking. 'We've met Colin Littlewood already.'

They rushed to the cemetery and to the place where they'd been standing for Freeman's burial.

'Where was he?' Monteith looked at the headstones.

'Over here, I think.' Watson shouted as he ran from headstone to headstone.

'I've found it. Over here, guv,' Monteith called out, 'Jackie Littlewood's headstone.'

Watson weaved through the lines of graves to where Monteith was standing. 'It *was* him. We spoke to him,' Watson said, frustrated.

'He knew why we were here; he knew Freeman was being buried that day. The bastard,' Monteith spat.

Watson read the inscription on her headstone.

Her Life a Beautiful Memory
Her Absence a Silent Grief

'More like a simmering grief, ' Watson mumbled.

———

Dumping her dad's Skoda and hiring a 4x4 in her mother's maiden name had been a great idea, Susan thought.

They'd left the Skoda in a supermarket car park, unlocked and with the keys in the driver's footwell. It would soon be spotted, but they would be long gone before that happened. An hour later, they pulled into the woodland holiday park.

Susan had booked a log cabin deep in the woods for a week. They would not be staying for that long, just a couple of days. The next stage needed to be planned thoroughly. If they had stayed at home, their nosy neighbours might've disturbed them.

The Banks were a lovely couple, and she and her father were indebted to them, but sometimes, they could be a real pain. Spending time away, just father and daughter, would give them some time to relax. No one to bother them.

After unpacking, Susan and her father stood on the sundeck with a soft drink, taking in the scenery. The lay out of the holiday park was one reason they'd chosen it. None of the cabins could be seen by the others.

Ducks were wandering around as if they owned the place, coming close, already knowing that the visitors would feed them. The surrounding trees were full of birds chirping and squawking, seeing who could be the loudest. Susan spotted a couple of squirrels scurrying up and down a tree, playing and looking for food. She pointed them out to her father, who chuckled. Something he had not done for a long time.

Littlewood sat back on one of the wooden chairs on the decking and closed his eyes, taking in the sun. Susan, sipping her drink, leant against the fence which surrounded the decking, looked at him and smiled. The contentment on his face was a joy to see. Susan smiled as she looked at him fondly. She'd do anything for her father.

CHAPTER TWELVE

'You are sure we've got this correct?' Matthews asked as Watson stuck the pictures of Colin Littlewood and his daughter Susan on the information board.

'Yes. We are positive Colin Littlewood killed Freeman, Davis and Knowles,' Watson replied confidently. 'He killed Freeman because he had a run in with him in Claythorn. Littlewood bust his nose because of what he said about his wife's, Jackie's, death. Also, because of what Freeman was in prison for. He turned up at Freeman's funeral; we even spoke to him, not knowing who he was. Knowles because he was Littlewood's boss, who sacked him with no regard for all he had been through. And Davis, for what he had been in prison for. Could have been shooting his mouth off while he was in there. Getting revenge for what he had to put up with while he was working there, vigilante killing.'

'Pity we can't let him continue.' Monteith let out a sigh.

'Only you could say something like that,' Crompton said, shaking his head. He caught Matthews doing the same.

'I know, bad taste,' Monteith continued, 'But it's what most of the public think. Prison is too good for some of these creeps. Davis was the biggest one.'

'Do we know who killed Littlewood's wife? Are they still inside?' Matthews asked, still shaking his head.

'I contacted Claythorn an hour ago, but they have not got back to us as yet,' Lorimer chipped in.

'Press them for an answer *now*. It's imperative we know. For their safety,' Crompton added. 'If they are out, we need to warn and protect them.'

Lorimer's phone rang. 'Yes.... Where? Are you sure it's his? Thank you, can you hang on?' He turned towards the others. 'That was the control room. They have stopped Littlewood's car for speeding in the town centre. Asked what you want them to do next?'

'Hold them and we will be there ASAP.' Watson and Monteith grabbed their jackets and ran towards the door.

'Text us the position, will you?' Monteith shouted.

Within ten minutes, they had pulled up behind the squad car and Freeman's car. Traffic around them had slowed down, obviously trying to see what was going on. As if this was the first time someone was being pulled over by the police.

Watson and Monteith looked at each other as they approached the cars. Something wasn't right. 'They're still in the car,' one of the uniformed officers said. 'He has failed a breath test and there is a strong smell of cannabis.'

Watson knocked on the driver's side window. The window was wound down. Staring at him was a thin, haggard looking man. Not Littlewood. The guy stank of alcohol and cannabis, as did the girl sitting next to him.

'Can I help you, officer?' The man slurred his words; he was barely understandable.

'Is this your car, sir?' Watson, annoyed, tried to keep his calm.

'Yes, it's my car. We have just been shopping. I told the officer that,' the driver replied matter-of-factly. There were Tesco shopping bags on the back seat. Cans of beer had spilt out and a bottle of vodka could be seen.

'Can I see your driving licence, please?'

'Err. I must have left it at home. I can bring it around later?'

Watson had had enough. He told the officers to arrest the couple, then walked away angrily.

Lorimer printed off the information he had just received from Claythorn prison, re-read it and headed to Crompton's office.

Crompton waved Lorimer in as he closed a file on his computer.

'Just heard from the prison. Littlewood's wife's killers Andrew McNulty and Thomas Smith are still in there. But they are due to be released soon,' Lorimer said as he stood by Crompton's desk.

'Did they say when?' Matthews asked

'No. They refused to give that info to a mere junior like me. Something about data protection?'

'Give me the phone number. I'll rattle their cage.' Lorimer handed the note to Crompton. 'Any news from the daring duo?'

'It was Littlewood's car, but a couple of druggies stole it from a supermarket car park. Uniform are bringing them in now.' Lorimer left Crompton's office.

Crompton opened the bottom draw of his desk and took out a bottle of Scotch and two glasses.

'Bit early, Kenneth?' Matthews raised his bushy eyebrows.

'Only medicinal. After the day we've had...' Crompton pushed a glass across the table.

Matthews took it, swirled the whisky around and took a sip. 'Nice.'

'So what are we going to do with Monteith?' Crompton eased his chair back and came round his desk, sitting next to Matthews.

'Besides shoot him for being a moron?'

'Well, I hadn't thought of that, but I suppose that could be arranged.'

'Joking aside,' Matthews said, taking another sip. 'I will deal with the editor of the newspaper. When he's made aware that certain doors will be closed if they run this casino story, I hope to persuade him to change his mind. As for Monteith,' he looked at the contents of his glass, 'I have an idea. We desperately need someone to be our ears and eyes with regard to Jimmy Russell. Since Monteith has established contact with him... '

Crompton's eyes shot open. '*What?* You want to use Monteith as bait? Grant, are you serious?'

'He already knows Russell. If he could get closer? See what else Russell is planning.'

Crompton wasn't convinced. 'I don't know if he's that close to Russell. He owes him money, but he is not friendly with him.'

'Maybe it's time for him to get closer?'

Crompton got up, pacing up and down. 'Do you honestly believe he will go for it? I don't.'

Matthews looked at Crompton with a knowing smile as he, too, got up out of his chair. 'Well, think about it. If that's all, I have to sort some things upstairs. By the way, that whisky is damn good. We must be paying you too much.' He went out of the door and walked straight into Monteith and Watson.

'He's done a runner. The bastard's done a runner.' Watson threw his jacket down over his seat. 'He's dumped his car and is laughing at us because we can't catch him.' Watson's frustration was boiling over.

Matthews stopped. 'Anything caught on the CCTV at the supermarket?'

'No, that's where we have just been. You can see Littlewood park his car and go into the supermarket, but we lost him in the crowd. Don't know where he went after. If he got into another vehicle waiting for him, we didn't see it.' Watson was grabbing a drink and something to eat as he filled Matthews in.

Monteith continued, slumped in his chair. 'His daughter's car was still in the driveway when we interviewed the next-door neighbours, Mr and Mrs Banks, so they are not using that one. They must have got another from somewhere. A rental?'

Matthews nodded. 'That sounds worth checking up. Good work. Keep me updated.' He paced out of the office.

Monteith and Watson stared. They looked at each other. 'Did that just happen? Matthews handing out a compliment?'

Tuesday

One thing detectives hate is early morning call outs. Even more so when it's raining. This morning at 6 a.m., it was pouring down.

An hour before, a call had come in from a dog-walking insomniac who had been walking along the river near the weir. He had spotted something tangled in the river's undergrowth.

Watson and Monteith stood on the riverside in their waterproof macs and wellingtons, under the bright lights of the arc lamps, looking like two drowned rats. Neither wanted to be there.

Across the river, about half a mile down from the weir, specialist police divers from the Underwater Search Unit had released the remains of a human body from the undergrowth and weeds. The rain had caused the river level to rise. The weir was flowing fast, making the extraction difficult.

The divers hauled the body into their boat and brought it over to the other bank. Twenty minutes later, the bloated body was on the grassy riverbank, laid out on a sheet of plastic. Its macabre state was enough to turn the stomach of the best rescue workers, but Mac was in his element, giving it the once over before taking it back to the morgue.

Mac's assistant was busy taking photos of the body, recording the state they found it in. It still had its running shirt, shorts and trainers on. But because of the bloating, they were tight and close to splitting.

Watson stood close by, but Monteith had had enough. One sight of the body and he had stepped back. Far back.

'I can't do a lot at the moment with the body,' Mac said to Watson, 'I have to wait until the air and methane gas come out before I can start the autopsy. What I can tell you is that the body is male and it has two bullet holes in it.'

'Bullet wounds! So it was murder. Can't give us a time of death?'

'Nope. Not until the post mortem later. Bodies in water react differently during decomposition, which makes timelines difficult to work out.' Mac turned to his assistants. 'Ok, you can bag him up now.' He walked back towards the weir with Watson and Monteith. Further down the river, the Underwater Search Unit were checking over their equipment.

Watson looked around as they approached the weir. 'If he didn't go in where we found the body, where did the murderer drop him?'

'Judging from the flow of the river, anywhere from the weir downwards. But that's for you to work out. I only deal with the bodies,' Mac replied cheerily.

———

Crompton was waiting for Watson in the office. He was speaking animatedly to Lorimer, who was updating the board with photographs and details.

'It's nice of you to join us. Did you have a good early morning walk by the river?'

'It was definitely murder, boss. Two bullet wounds. But otherwise... it was lovely boss, you should have joined us. Walking in the rain with the one you love,' Watson said, staring longingly at Monteith.

'Well, Terry, *guv*, you say the nicest things.' Monteith batted his eyes at Watson while giving him a peck on the cheek.

'So the Secret Policeman's Ball is alive and well then?' Crompton stifled a laugh. 'Listen, we have some new information. I would like to introduce you to Andrew McNulty and Thomas Smith.' He pointed to the new photos on the board.

'These two lovely people killed Littlewood's wife, and are due to be released from Claythorn this Friday. We need to be there before

Littlewood and take them into protective custody. I can't stress enough that we need to get this right. I don't want this bastard killing anyone else. He's been one step ahead of us, but now we can stop him. I have spoken to the governor of Claythorn and arranged for McNulty and Smith to be handed over to us before they leave. Watson, arrange that they are picked up on Friday and brought back here.'

'Have we any idea where Littlewood and his daughter are now?' Watson asked.

Lorimer chipped in. 'No, looks like he has gone to ground somewhere. After ditching his car and leaving his daughter's at home, we don't know what they're driving now. All rental places we have talked to don't recognise him and have no record of a Littlewood renting a car.'

Crompton added, 'An APB has been put out already, so we should get word as soon as there's any sight of him.' His phone started ringing. 'Excuse me.'

'So when are you two moving in together?' Lorimer said mischievously.

'When our divorces come through, sweetheart,' Monteith replied. 'But sorry, hon, you're not my type,' he added as he blew Lorimer a kiss.

Crompton reappeared from his office. 'Right, Watson, Matthews wants to see you in his office.'

'In his office? What for?' Watson looked quizzical. Crompton shot him a knowing glance. 'Oh right,' Watson mumbled.

After taking the lift to the fourth floor, they walked along the corridor and into Matthews' outer office. His secretary, Beryl, stared at them over her glasses, with a face that looked like she was sucking a lemon. 'Go straight in, he's expecting you.'

Matthews was sitting behind his large desk, typing on his keyboard. To his left was a bookcase which stretched the length of the wall. It contained books, files, and personal items. In front of the desk were three leather-backed wooden chairs.

'Sit down. I won't be a minute.' Matthews finished typing and clicked a few things with the mouse.

'Right, gentlemen. Following the incident at the casino the other night... Yes, I have seen the CCTV. I have managed to put out the fire. But, DCI Watson, even though it seems you are not responsible for what happened, I am disappointed at your managerial skills. Why didn't I see a report of this incident? Why wasn't DS Monteith disciplined? You are a DCI and I expect you to be able to control your people. Now, I need your assurance that this will *not* happen again. Do I have your guarantee you will handle your team?'

Watson hesitated, then said, 'With all due respect, sir, I hear what you are saying and yes, Monteith overstepped the line. But... he's my best friend and I know he is under a lot of pressure lately. This was a one-off and I'm positive it won't happen again. Monteith is a good detective, as you know.'

Matthews did not look convinced but continued, 'Okay, let's leave that in the past for now then. Especially since I want to inform you of a proposal I will put before Monteith.' He outlined what he and Crompton had discussed earlier.

Watson looked shocked. 'You cannot be serious, sir. The situation is dangerous enough for Monteith.'

'I hear what you are saying, DCI Watson, but I didn't ask you here to discuss the proposal,' Matthews said sternly. 'Consider yourself hereby informed. Now, be so good as to get DS Monteith into my office.'

Speechless, Watson opened his mouth, then shut it. His face looked grim as he went out to fetch Monteith.

'Right DS Monteith, as I've mentioned to your superiors, I've managed to suppress spreading of the CCTV of you beating up your DCI at the casino. As you can understand, I was shocked to see you lose your temper in such a way, and the disrespect you showed DCI Watson.'

Monteith tried to speak, but Matthews stopped him. 'Don't thank me. This will be put on your record and I'm sure DCI Watson will keep you on a short leash from now on. If it were me, I'd demoted you back to uniform, walking the beat until your feet feel sore. But both your superiors have put in a good word for you.'

'Thank you, sir,' Monteith mumbled, looking sideways at Watson.

Matthews continued, 'Put that aside, your connection with Jimmy Russell, one of the biggest crooks we have here, could be of value. As I said, there will be repercussions. However, you know as well as anyone that we never had a chance to get close to Jimmy Russell, one of the biggest crooks we have here.'

Watson was feeling uncomfortable. He hoped Monteith would reject Matthews' proposal. He would, he thought.

'DS Monteith, we want you to get close to Jimmy Russell. You've already seen inside his casino, spoken to him, shared a table with him, so you're the best person we know who could do this.'

Monteith's mouth fell open. 'You cannot be serious, sir. You've suppressed the scandal the newspaper could cause, but this? I take it that if I don't do this, I'm demoted or out of the job. You're putting a target on my back and hanging me out to dry,' he exclaimed.

Matthews shook his head. 'No, sergeant, this will be your choice only. We would very much like you to help us out here but understand the danger. However, we feel this opportunity is too good to miss, hence the proposal. We've been waiting for years to get a grip on Russell and you might just be the person who can bring him down.'

Concerned for his friend, Watson looked at Monteith, who was staring into a void, it seemed. *Would he accept? Say no*, he thought.

After what seemed ages, Monteith sighed deeply. He focused on Matthews, ignoring Watson's eyes. 'I'll do it, sir.'

Tuesday Evening

Monteith sat in his car, his stomach turning somersaults. Each half of his brain felt like it was throwing punches against the other in a WWE fight. On the seat next to him was an envelope containing five grand, a loan coming out of his monthly payment. Matthews had signed off on it as it was the perfect excuse for Monteith to go back to Jimmy Russell. Five grand, he thought bitterly, coming with strings attached. What a mess he'd got himself into. All because of his gambling habit.

He had phoned ahead, making sure Jimmy Russell would be in. Now here he was, sat in front of the casino, contemplating his next move. Flight or fight.

As it was early evening, the casino was almost void of visitors. The high rollers would not come in until the late evening, spending enough to keep a small country out of debt. Standing just inside the doors were the same two bouncers who'd escorted him last time. They already knew why he was there.

As they came out of the lift, Jimmy Russell was in deep conversation with his brother Allan, looking at a large sheet of paper and pointing as they looked over the balcony at the casino floor below.

'Mr Monteith, please join us.' Jimmy Russell beckoned him over. Monteith took a tentative step forward. Russell put his arm around his shoulder.

'We were discussing making some changes. Adding more things in, fruit machines, another blackjack table. We are also thinking of adding a men-only club in a room at the back. Maximising revenue streams, what do you think?'

'Err, I don't know. If you think you need to, then go ahead,' Monteith stuttered.

'See, Allan? Even Mr Monteith here thinks it's a good idea.' Russell slapped Monteith on the back. He continued, sharply now, 'But that's not why you're here.'

Monteith dug around in his jacket, pulling out the envelope of money. 'It's all there, your five grand.'

Russell took the envelope and opened it. He smiled coldly, then signalled to the bouncers. They grabbed Monteith under the arms, holding him tight. Monteith struggled, in vain.

'Thank you, Mr Monteith. Now, that was easy, wasn't it?' Russell patted him on the cheek. 'See Mr Monteith back to his car, lads. Oh, and... this time, be careful.' Russell pocketed the envelope and walked off with his brother to his inner sanctum.

CHAPTER THIRTEEN

Wednesday Morning

THE MORTUARY WAS BECOMING a second home for Watson and Monteith lately. This morning, they were present to attend the autopsy of the body that had been fished out of the river.

Mac and his assistant were dressed in all their finery, green scrubs, yellow wellies and gloves, plus masks which looked like they came from the local welders.

Both the detectives, standing well back from the table, were kitted out in the same gear except for the gloves and masks. They had paper masks on. Even with those, the stench radiating from the body was terrible. It was all too much for Monteith, who emptied the contents of his breakfast into a nearby sink before staggering out of the door, his face the colour of his scrubs.

After cutting away the body's clothes and giving it a clean, Mac bowed over the chest and examined it closely.

Mac's assistant took photos of the victim's chest. Watson approached the table, his hand holding his mask closer to his face, trying to minimise the smell.

Mac pointed to two holes in the chest. 'There are the two bullet wounds. He was dead when he ended up in the river, no water in his lungs. I will see if the bullets are still in there when I open him up.'

'I take it there was no ID on him?'

'No, I will have to use his teeth for ID. Fish and other wildlife have eaten his fingertips, along with other parts of his body.'

Mac showed the damaged fingers, ears and lips. The body moaned as trapped gases escaped. Watson backed away from the table as the stench grew more pungent.

'Jesus, that's rank. How can you work on a body like this?'

'Luckily, we don't get many bloaters, but you get used to it after a while. The fire victims are the worst. It takes forever to get the smell of smoke and burnt flesh out of here. The sales of air fresheners go up when we have one of them,' Mac said.

'I will check missing persons' reports. Somebody has to be wondering where he is. Thanks, Mac.' Watson started towards the door. He could feel his own stomach groaning.

'Don't you want to stay for the examination?' Mac asked, holding a scalpel. 'I was just about to cut him open.'

'To quote you: you only do the bodies; we work out the rest.'

Littlewood and Susan were relaxing at their woodland retreat.

They sunbathed on the decking, walked along the miles of woodland trails, and even did a spot of swimming in the camp's indoor pool. Susan noticed she was being eyed up by some of young men trying to outdo each other, posing around the sides of the pool. Flattered by all the attention, she wished it were at a different time and place. Littlewood had also observed this. He smiled with pride, his daughter being the centre of attention for once.

She'd had a crap upbringing. He knew that. Helping a depressive alcoholic after her mother's murder was something no child should have to go through. But she had, and she was now a beautiful young woman.

'Why don't you go and enjoy yourself?' Littlewood suggested, as she came back to the table.

'No! I came with you. We are on holiday together.' Susan was adamant.

'Listen, I will be all right. Tomorrow, we have a big day. You need to let your hair down. You've been looking after me for years. It's time you did something for yourself.'

'But Dad...'

'No buts.' Littlewood put a hand on her arm and spoke softly. 'I've seen those guys over there looking at you. Talk to them, enjoy yourself. I will be fine.'

Susan leant over and kissed him on his forehead. 'Thanks, Dad.'

She went back to the cabin to change out of her swimwear into a nice, flowery summer dress and headed back. Walking around the holiday site, she took everything in. They had been to other camps before, but that was when her mother was alive. Now, for the first time since those happy days, she felt alive again. Free, if only for a few hours.

When Watson and Monteith arrived back at the station, Monteith ran towards the toilets, feeling sick again. *Those bloody autopsies*, he thought, *I should be able to hold myself together better.* Now Watson had had to drive his car as he felt too queasy to drive. He sighed and splashed water on his face.

'Where's Keith?' Lorimer asked when Watson walked into the office, alone. He was at his computer with Crompton looking through the latest missing persons list.

'Kermit's in the toilet groaning down the big white telephone. That last body really turned his stomach.'

'Kermit?' Lorimer laughed heartily. 'It was that bad?'

'Oh yes. Even I struggled, but survived,' Watson grinned. 'How are you doing with missing persons?'

'We have only just started. There's a few out there, but none at the moment matches our body. We might have to wait until Mac has done his business.'

Watson nodded, then sighed. 'I had better see how Keith is,' he said as he walked towards the toilets.

Monteith was washing his face when he entered. 'How are you, Keith?'

Monteith grabbed a handful of paper towels. 'I'll be fine, guv. Just give me ten minutes.'

'No, you still look green to me. I am ordering you to take the rest of the day off.'

'No, I'm fine.'

'That's an order. You are not much good to me in the state you're in. Go home.'

Monteith shrugged his shoulders and nodded.

'One more thing,' Watson said as they walked out of the toilet, 'Did you pay off Russell last night?

'Yes, I paid him. He was discussing something with his brother when I got there. I didn't stay too long. His goons threw me out.'

'Did you catch what they were discussing?'

'Catch it? He told me! They are going to expand the casino. Bringing in a men-only club.' Monteith's face paled. His stomach was playing up again.

'Interesting. Right, you get off now. Don't come back until the morning.' He escorted Monteith to the lift and sent him on his way.

Early Thursday Morning

Littlewood and Susan packed up their things and started their journey back to Ravenswood. Dawn was breaking, and the sun shone brightly, lighting their way to their final destination. The beauty of renting a 4x4 instead of using either of their cars was that no one would look for this car, and hopefully slip back into the city unnoticed. Keeping off the main roads added to their safety.

They didn't speak. They didn't need to. That had been done in the cabin, father and daughter. Between them, they'd worked out their revenge plan.

It was a bit like entering the lion's den. Would they be able to get to McNulty and Smith without raising suspicion? Would they bump into someone from Claythorn who'd recognise them? Now they'd come this far, they *had* to see it through. Their ultimate act of revenge.

Littlewood pulled into the visitors car park, parking close so they could get in and out quickly. That was the plan. Would it work? Littlewood looked at Susan. He smiled at his daughter. 'Thank you for everything.' A tear rolled down his cheek.

'Your loss is mine, Dad, as is your revenge.' Susan wiped the tear away and kissed him on the cheek. She got out and waited on the path, away from the others, waiting for their loved ones.

The pickup was easier than they'd thought.

When they came out, Susan strolled towards them with a big smile. 'Hi guys, great you're out.' Smith and McNulty looked surprised but let Susan hug them. She threw her arms around McNulty and stuck the gun in his ribs. 'Don't do anything stupid,' she whispered, 'And don't think I would hesitate to kill you. Now, walk.' The two men looked shocked, panic on their faces.

Susan glanced around, on alert, as they trudged to the 4x4. The gun steady in her hand. Littlewood had already opened the back door.

His face grim, he gripped Smith first and bound his hands together with tie-wraps, then pushed him in the car and proceeded with McNulty. He shoved the door closed and got in the driver's seat. Littlewood drove slowly out of the car park, trying to not attract attention from other released inmates and their families.

McNulty protested, 'You cannot do this! We are free men now. Let us out.' Smith just nodded, fear etched on his face.

'Shut up,' Susan said, turning around and pointing her gun at the men in the back seat.

Littlewood headed for an area on the edge of the city that comprised wasteland and disused industrial buildings. A brownfield area down for redevelopment, but nothing had started yet. The perfect place to exact vengeance.

He pulled into one of the derelict warehouses and parked up.

McNulty and Smith had stayed quiet, but now they started protesting again. 'You cannot do this. Let us go! You freaking idiots, let us go!'

Littlewood ignored their accusations. He jumped out, opened the rear door and pulled a screaming McNulty out, dragging him around the back of the 4x4. Susan, brandishing the gun, ordered Smith out of the other side, forcing them to kneel next to each other in the dirt and rubbish on the floor.

Littlewood paced slowly in front of McNulty and Smith. 'Let me introduce myself. My name is Colin Littlewood, and this is my daughter. You murdered my wife and Susan's mother when you robbed our place ten years ago. You think you got away with it. You think you got your reprieve. Think again.'

'We didn't,' McNulty said with vehemence, but unable to hide the fear in his voice. 'We just went in to rob the place.'

'Shut up,' Littlewood roared. 'I don't want to hear your snivelling or pity. It won't help where you are going.'

'She fell. We didn't touch her,' Smith shouted.

Susan pointed the gun at him. 'Did you not hear my father? Shut up.'

'You were still in our house. You were *robbing* us, scumbags. If you were not in our house, she would not have died. YOU KILLED MY WIFE.' Littlewood's face was just inches away from Smith's. He was looking straight into the frightened man's eyes.

Smith turned his face away, eyes tight shut. Littlewood raged with anger and punched him twice in the face. Smith howled in pain, his nose dripping blood.

Littlewood then lashed out and kicked McNulty in the stomach, making him keel over sideways, coughing and gasping for air. An enraged Littlewood dragged him back up and punched him in his face, over and over.

Susan looked at her father and recognised the hate in his eyes. He was executing his revenge, at last, for her mother's death. He had waited ten years for this moment. Killing Freeman, Davis and Knowles had only been foreplay. This was what they had planned all along.

'You're a nutter, a lunatic. You're the one that should be locked up,' Smith shouted.

Littlewood, fury in his eyes, kicked him in the stomach and kept hitting his face. Smith tried to cover his face with his hands, but they were still tied. Littlewood grabbed him by the hair and pulled him up.

'Dad!' Susan was now concerned. Her father seemed out of control. 'Enough now, Dad, please. Let's finish this.'

Littlewood looked dazed. He straightened his back and looked at her with a glazed-over look in his eyes, puffing hard, trying to get his breath back.

Susan handed him the gun.

Littlewood looked at the weapon and then at McNulty and Smith. Both were staring back at him, panic-stricken. He stepped forward and placed the gun on McNulty's forehead. McNulty screamed in terror. Littlewood slowly pulled the gun away. Then he placed it on Smith's forehead. Smith wriggled, trying to get away.

Littlewood lifted his arm high and hit him on the head with the gun. Blood started rolling down Smith's face.

'Dad, shoot them!' Susan stressed. She didn't like seeing her father like this, it was scaring. 'This is not what we agreed on, Dad. Just shoot them so we can leave.'

Littlewood glared at Susan, a cold look in his eyes. He shook his head. 'No, no, Susan. We won't kill them here. Shooting's too good for them. I want them to suffer like your mother suffered. I have a better idea.'

'What are you talking about, Dad? We had it all sorted!' Susan was panicking.

Littlewood gave a little laugh. 'Get them back into the 4x4. We are going for a little drive.'

'Where? Tell me, Dad? I'm getting worried.'

Littlewood walked across to Susan and put his hand on her cheek. 'The multi-storey. Chucking them off the top of that, falling to their death like your mother did, seems a fitting end for them.'

'But... Dad?'

Littlewood shot a warning glance at her. 'You not behind me anymore? Remember, my revenge is yours. That's what you said.'

'Yes. Yes, I'm always with you. It's just we had a plan. Now we're so close, you want to change it?'

'Right, stop it and get them in the car. You're driving.' He threw the keys at her and shoved McNulty and Smith back in the car. He threw them on the floor so no one could see them. They moaned in pain. Quickly, Littlewood put masking tape over their mouths and then couldn't help himself. He punched them again, in the stomach, and kicked them when he closed the door and climbed into the passenger seat.

Susan fired up the engine and started driving back into the city. She didn't know what to make of her father. He had done a complete U-turn. From the man who had organised the murders and his revenge meticulously to this out-of-control raging machine.

She looked across at him. He was calm, as if out for a Sunday drive. But she spotted the manic look in his eyes, his legs twitching, stroking the gun like it was a pet.

Then it all went horribly wrong.

They pulled up for the traffic lights. Beside them, a police car drew up. One officer looked at them, then nudged his partner. Littlewood smiled disarmingly and wound down his window. The officers smiled back. They didn't have an inkling what would happen next. Littlewood raised his arm and fired at the car. The blast took out the windscreen.

Susan stared in disbelief, eyes wide open.

'DRIVE, DRIVE, DRIVE!!' her father shouted.

Shaken with fear, Susan slammed the car into gear and floored it.

Wheels screeching, the 4x4 launched forward. Susan managed not to hit anything as they took off the road like a scalded cat.

'What the hell did you do that for?' Susan shouted back at her father.

'They had recognised us.'

'You don't know that! For Christ's sake, you did not have to shoot them.' Susan was looking in her rear-view mirror, checking no one followed them.

'Shut up and get us to the multi-storey.'

CHAPTER FOURTEEN

'Hey Karl, when do you take your sergeant's exam? It must be soon,' Watson asked, as he walked past Lorimer's desk, heading for another coffee refill.

'In a month,' Lorimer replied, leaning back in his chair. 'Was up till one this morning revising.'

'If you need help, you only need to ask,' Watson added.

'Cheers, it's been...' Lorimer paused, choosing his words carefully, 'entertaining, interesting, seeing how you work.'

Monteith laughed. Getting up, he joined Watson at Lorimer's desk. 'That's you being told off, guv.'

'Helping with this investigation has made me more determined to become a detective sergeant,' Lorimer smiled.

'Good to hear,' Watson replied, 'because I have heard that the bosses are looking to have another detective joining our team. They are interviewing newly trained detective constables.'

A bang made them look up. They turned around to see Crompton slamming his fists hard onto his desk.

'Wonder who's upset the boss,' Monteith mused as they heard him turning the air blue with expletives.

Watson nodded towards Crompton's office. 'Looks like we're going to find out.'

Crompton stormed out of his office, banging the door shut with force.

'They were released this morning,' Crompton exclaimed. His face was red with rage. 'They fucking released McNulty and Smith this morning!'

'What do you mean this morning? We were told it would be tomorrow.' Monteith, who had been taking a sip of his coffee, coughed and spluttered.

'I've just got off the phone with the governor. They released McNulty and Smith at 8 a.m.'

Watson looked at his watch. Nine thirty. 'They could be anywhere by now,' he said, frustrated. 'Who picked them up? Their families?'

'Don't have a clue. The governor didn't know. He was in a meeting. Seems once they are out of their front gates, they're not the prison's problem.' Crompton was fuming. 'I've told him we want to see CCTV coverage of their front gate as soon as possible. If not, I will charge him with obstruction of a police investigation.' Crompton grabbed his coat, sending the coat stand flying. 'I'm going there straight away. Watson, Monteith, you are coming with me. You can stop me from hitting him.'

Twenty minutes later, Crompton's anger hadn't subsided. He was on a warpath and the governor of Claythorn prison was in his sights. Nothing Monteith and Watson said during the drive calmed their boss down.

As soon as Monteith parked up in the visitors car park, Crompton jumped out and stormed up the path leading to the main door. Watson was half out of the car. 'Boss, boss, wait, calm down.'

He caught up with Crompton as he opened the door into the reception. 'Boss, hang on.'

Crompton let go of the door. 'What?'

'Just calm down. They won't let you see anyone if you go in there like Storming Norman. This is not your territory, and you cannot throw your weight around.'

Crompton pointed towards the door. 'But they have just released two men, possibly into the arms of a raging psycho. What the hell were they doing?'

'Their job,' Watson replied dryly.

Monteith joined them at the door. 'Just to let you know, we are being watched.' Looking up, they saw the CCTV camera above them. 'They have focused on you two since you started.'

That didn't help Crompton's anger.

Watson took control. 'Please, boss, just compose yourself. I will book us in.' Approaching the reception desk, he introduced himself to one of the security officers behind the security glass. 'DSI Crompton, DS Monteith and DCI Watson to see Governor Greenslade. We are expected.' They showed their IDs.

They were escorted upstairs and into a side office, fitted out with CCTV monitors and recording equipment. Two officers sat in front of the bank of equipment. The screens showed every part of the prison.

'Where is he?' Crompton mumbled under his breath, watching the daily routine and ritual of prison life.

'Be patient.' Watson knew his boss was still on a short fuse.

The door opened and in strode Governor Greenslade, a blue manila folder in his hand. He looked like a headmaster of old. Greying hair, rounded metal glasses, a shirt and tie, jumper, and checked jacket.

'Sorry to keep you waiting, gentlemen. My secretary unexpectedly took a few days off, and I have had trouble finding the relevant paperwork. I had to rearrange an important meeting because of this.' He turned towards the prison officers. 'Have we got the CCTV footage from this morning?'

'Yes, sir, it's all set up.'

'Who was it you were interested in, Detective Superintendent?'

'Mr Greenslade,' Crompton said through gritted teeth. 'I am sorry we have ruined your morning, but we believe two of your former guests are in danger. AND we would like to find out why they were released twenty-four hours before the date we were told, and who picked them up. Now if it's not too much trouble, we would like to see the footage urgently. I hope you have a good explanation for what the hell went on.' He stopped, out of breath. In his outburst, he'd moved so close to Greenslade that he could count the hairs in his nose.

Greenslade looked taken aback. He stuttered, 'Err... right.. Okay... mmm. Can we see the pictures, Craig?'

The prison officer showed the men a clip of fourteen men milling inside the reception area, ready to be released. Some were by themselves, some were talking. Others were pacing around, eager to get out and into the arms of their loved ones.

'Which ones are McNulty and Smith?' Watson asked the prison officer.

'They're the two in the back corner,' the officer called Craig, pointed. They were not talking to anyone, keeping to themselves.

'Do inmates get released every day?' Watson was intrigued.

'Yes, except for weekends and bank holidays. If their release date falls on one of those days, they go on a Friday.'

'Is there a limit to the number you release at the same time?'

'No. If it's your time, you go. You could be the only one that day. Or you could be part of a large group like this one.'

Watson looked closer at the prisoners being released. 'Hey Keith, have a look at this. Isn't that Justin Taylor?'

Monteith joined them and looked at the man.

'Yes, my God. Didn't we put him away for those jewellery raids five years ago? And look, there's Darren Barnes. He was done for glassing that bloke in the Carpenters Arms. I remember,' Monteith added, 'GBH wasn't it, after the bloke lost an eye in the attack?'

'When you two have stopped playing guess the crime, looks like they are on the way out. Now concentrate,' Crompton admonished his detectives. He was still on gas mark 4, simmering but close to the boil.

The next scene saw the inmates walking out of the reception towards the large metal front gate. The time on the tape read 8 a.m. McNulty and Smith were still at the back, keeping their distance. The CCTV footage switched to outside the gate. Relatives were gathered there, waiting for their loved ones to be released. A row of taxis was waiting close by.

The gate slid back slowly on its rollers. Red lights attached to the nearby wall flashed, and a siren blasted out. Before the gate was fully open, the ex-inmates were pouring out, running towards their family. Some went straight through and walked out.

'Probably wanting to get as far away from Claythorn as possible,' Monteith remarked.

Crompton studied the screen. 'Where are McNulty and Smith?'

'They have just come out, bottom left of the screen,' Watson pointed out.

'Don't lose them.'

Smith and McNulty turned out of the gate and started to walk across the prison's car park. Suddenly, a woman came up to them and hugged them.

Crompton exclaimed, 'Who is that woman? Does anybody know?' He was getting wound up again.

'That's Susan Farmer, my PA.' Greenslade's voice was filled with shock.

They all turned to look at him.

'*That* is your PA?' Crompton was confused.

Greenslade nodded, just as confused. 'Yes. She rang in yesterday, saying she was taking a few days off. She was going away with her father because he was not well.'

'Well, it looks like she's not gone anywhere,' Crompton snapped. 'How does she know McNulty and Smith?'

'I don't know, honestly.'

'Look at this.' Watson had kept watching the CCTV images. Susan was now escorting McNulty and Smith through the visitors car park.

They watched as Susan Farmer made Smith and McNulty go towards a 4x4. A man got out of the car and fiddled with each of the men, then pushed them into the back of the car.

'Is there another CCTV in the visitors car park, so we can see what went on?'

'I will check.' Craig pushed a few buttons.

Crompton chose that time to let rip at the governor. 'Right, Mr Greenslade, how the hell did they get released twenty-four hours before they should have? Any ideas please, because I'm damned if I'm leaving this — especially after what I have just seen.'

'I have CCTV from the visitors car park,' Craig exclaimed. Monteith and Watson stood looking over Craig's shoulders at the screens.

'I've not finished,' Crompton warned Greenslade.

The first couple of minutes showed what they had already seen, albeit from a different angle. But from this angle, it was clear that she had pulled out a gun while hugging them.

Watson pointed to the screen, '*Now* we know why they went with her. She threatened them. She's got them at bloody gun-point. Didn't anyone see this happen?'

Both the officers on the CCTV equipment shook their heads.

Back on the screen, Susan, McNulty and Smith had reached the 4x4. From this CCTV footage, they could identify the driver. 'That's Littlewood!' Watson exclaimed. 'Shit, they have McNulty and Smith.'

'That must be his daughter,' Monteith said, not wanting to believe what was playing out in front of him on the camera.

They watched as McNulty and Smith were shoved into the back of the 4x4. Susan was waving the gun in their faces before she got in.

The 4x4 then left the car park, heading toward the city centre, with Littlewood driving.

Monteith and Watson stood looking at each other, not daring to express their opinion.

Crompton broke the silence.

'Well, that was one big fuck up. And Greenslade, I am looking at the biggest fuck up here. This is entirely your fault. How were two inmates released 24 hours before their due date? And then walked straight into the hands of the two people who want them dead? I want to see the paperwork. I'm holding you responsible if anything happens to them.'

Greenslade slowly handed over the folder he had been holding. 'All the details are in there.'

Watson's phone rang; he went out of the room to take it.

Crompton opened the file and started reading. 'According to this official printout from your records, McNulty and Smith were due for release tomorrow. But the date on the copy of the release letters says the release date is today.'

'Who writes and sends out these letters?' Crompton waved them at Greenslade.

'Susan, my PA, once I have seen and confirmed the details of the Parole Board.'

'Your secretary, who we have just witnessed pointing a gun at Andrew McNulty and Thomas Smith. And you don't check these letters? They don't require your signature?'

'No, no need. I trusted Susan.'

Before Crompton could lose his temper again, Watson came flying back into the room.

'That was the control room. Littlewood's 4x4 was spotted by uniform, but Littlewood shot at their car as he took off, taking out the windscreen. Another squad car then saw Littlewood enter the multi-storey in the city centre. They believe he has driven up to the top level. Uniform have shut the multi-storey and are keeping their distance. They have called armed response.'

By the time they were out of the prison and back in Monteith's BMW, Crompton's frustration and anger had risen to another level. He was cursing and swearing at anything and everything. They received a police squad car escort to get them through the traffic for the last mile. The roads around the multi-storey had been closed off as a precaution. The multi-storey was a favourite place to jump off for the desperate and the despondent.

Monteith pulled up by the entrance. Lorimer was already there, talking to the emergency services. He saw them, jogged across, and jumped into the back.

'What's happening?' Crompton asked tersely.

'Littlewood's 4x4 was spotted about twenty minutes ago by two PCs in a squad car at traffic lights. Apparently, Littlewood opened the window and shot at them. Luckily, no officer got hit. Another car took up the pursuit. They took no attempt to stop him but followed at a safe distance to this car park, up onto the top level. Littlewood is parked at one end, the squad car at the other. They have not approached Littlewood and as far as I am aware, no one has got out of his 4x4. We have cleared the car park up to the level below. The cars are still on that and the top. The owners are being kept away from the area. Armed response has arrived and is on the level below, along with the hostage negotiator.' Lorimer's run-down was thorough.

They could hear a police helicopter flying over.

'Where is Matthews?' Crompton asked. 'I expected him to be here.'

'Still back at headquarters, but wanting to be kept in the loop.'

'At least that's some good news. Don't want him around bungling this up. Right, Keith, let's get up there and see what's happening.'

Monteith swung the car around and headed through the police cordon at the multi-storey entrance.

Driving slowly up the ramps onto the deserted levels was very eerie. Nobody in Monteith's car said anything, all looking at the vacant spaces in the concrete monolith. Normally they would be full of cars of shoppers and workers from the nearby offices, who had paid for weekly or monthly passes.

Monteith inched his car up onto the sixth level. They parked up and walked over to the head of the Armed Response Unit, who handed them flak jackets.

The ARU officer gave an update. 'The suspect's car has been static for about fifteen minutes at the far end of the level above. Looks like there are four people in the car, two in the front and two in the back. Not much movement in the back, but the two in the front have been in animated conversation.'

Crompton nodded, taking everything in. 'Can we get up on the next level?'

'Yes, I can take you up there, but we need to be cautious. We don't know what this Littlewood fella is going to do.' He nodded at Lorimer. 'We've been filled in on what happened earlier on. I don't want to take any chances. If I tell you to move back, you *will* do it.'

'Well done, Karl,' Crompton said. 'We'll make a detective out of you yet.'

Lorimer shrugged the compliment off, 'With you lot at the Claythorn, and the reports started coming in… Someone had to organise it all.'

Watson put a hand on Lorimer's shoulder. 'Word of advice. When someone, especially bosses, gives you a compliment, take it. They're not given out very often.'

'Are you ready?' the ARU officer asked.

'When you are,' Crompton replied.

Just as they started up the ramp, there was a cracking voice over the officer's radio. 'Movement at the car, repeat, movement at the car. Doors being opened.'

The ARU officer listened. 'Anybody getting out?'

'Two in front out. Opening back doors. Two people in the back being dragged out of the car. Looks like they are bound up.'

The ARU officer turned back to Crompton. 'You wanted to get closer. Let's move up, it's getting interesting. But remember, trouble and…'

Crompton nodded.

The ARU cautiously went up the last ramp onto the top level. They spaced out using the cars which had been trapped there as cover. Crompton, Watson, Monteith, and Lorimer came up behind and were told to stay back for now.

CHAPTER FIFTEEN

Littlewood and Susan were standing next to the 4x4, by the outside wall. Between them, on the ground, were McNulty and Smith. Below, the road leading to the car park was deserted. Police cars and tape blocked the way. The only cars visible were emergency vehicles.

Watson took a chance. Crouching down, he ran to get a better view from a nearby car closer to the action, but still behind the ARU.

'Where the hell are you going, guv?' Monteith hissed.

'I need to see what's going on.' Watson was on his knees behind the car, signalling for Monteith to join him. Watson stuck his head up, looking over the car's bonnet.

'What can you see?' Monteith asked.

'Littlewood and Susan are standing by the 4x4.'

'Any sign of McNulty and Smith?'

Waston struggled to see. 'No, I can only see... Wait, I see them. They're next to Littlewood on the ground. JESUS CHRIST!'

'What?' Monteith called, 'What happened?'

'Looks like they've been beaten. They have tape over their mouths and I think their hands are tied behind their backs.'

Crompton and Lorimer had come closer as well, hiding behind another car on the other side of the level.

'Are they still alive?' Monteith asked.

'Looks like it, but I can see blood on them. I think they're in a bad way.'

At the other end, father and daughter were arguing, oblivious to their surroundings.

'Dad, this is not what we agreed,' Susan was pleading. She grabbed hold of his arm.

He shrugged her off. 'Yes, well, I told you I had a better idea for these scumbags.' Littlewood kicked McNulty again, who whimpered in pain.

'Dad, please think...' Susan was crying now.

'I HAVE. I've had ten years of thinking. Ten years of thinking about your mother, about the life we all could have been living if not for these two bastards. Ten years thinking of what I'd do to them. Planning my revenge. Ten years thinking about this day. Ten wasted years.' Littlewood grabbed Thomas Smith and dragged him up, punching him in the stomach.

Smith collapsed on the ground.

'Colin Littlewood, Susan. This is the Ravenswood police. Please put down your weapons and release your hostages.' The voice of the hostage negotiator boomed out through a loudhailer.

It stopped Littlewood in his tracks. Susan froze.

Father and daughter looked in shock at the ARU officers, with firearms at the ready.

'Colin, please think of what you are doing. What do you want? How can we end this peacefully?' the negotiator tried again.

'I want revenge. JUSTICE FOR MY WIFE,' Littlewood shouted. 'I want these two miserable cowards to pay for what they did.'

Stealthily, Crompton had moved forward. He now grabbed the loudhailer.

'This is Detective Superintendent Crompton. Littlewood, give it up. You cannot get out of this. They *have* paid for what they did. In prison. Put your weapons down and release them.'

'NO. NO, NO,' Littlewood roared. He grabbed Smith's collar and his belt and lifted him up, pushing him towards the edge. Smith screamed out in panic.

'DAD, NO!' Susan blurted. 'I am not being a part of this. We had an agreement. I have had enough.' Looking scared and terrified, she turned around and ran towards the police. 'HELP. Please, don't shoot. I want...' she sobbed, tears streaming down her face.

'Stop right there. Down on the floor and hands on your head.'

Susan did as she was told.

Four ARU officers moved forward and surrounded her before pushing her flat on the ground. They cuffed her, lifted her, and took her away.

A burst of gunfire blasted through the air.

'Who fired? Who fired?' the head of the Armed Response Unit shouted. 'I gave no order to fire.'

Everyone looked around.

'Boss? What the hell are you doing?' Open-mouthed, Watson stared at Crompton who had a gun in his hands, the loudhailer on the floor beside him.

'Guv, look!' Monteith pointed.

Colin Littlewood was lying on the ground. McNulty and Smith were crouched by the wall. A small group of ARU officers made their way over to Littlewood. One checked Littlewood, feeling for a pulse. Three gunshot wounds were visible, one in the head and two in the body. The officer confirmed over the radio that Littlewood was dead.

'Boss, give me your gun,' Watson spoke slowly to Crompton. 'Boss, please.'

Crompton stood still, staring in front of him. He turned his head towards Watson. His eyes were glazed over.

'He wanted justice. I have given it to him,' Crompton said in a harsh tone. 'And justice for Elizabeth Preston.'

Watson remained calm. 'Boss, your gun, and please don't say anything else.'

Crompton nodded. He let the gun slip out of his hands. Watson took it and handed it over to an ARU officer, who placed it into an evidence bag.

Watson hesitated, then said, in a formal tone, 'Detective Superintendent Crompton, I am arresting you for the murder of Colin Littlewood. You do not have to say anything. But it may harm your defence if you do not mention when questioned something which you later rely on in court. Anything you do say may be given in evidence.'

'Do we *have* to read him his rights?' Monteith whispered.

Watson looked at him. 'I fear so.'

He guided Crompton to a waiting squad car and put him in the back seat. An eerie silence hung in the air as the car set off down the ramp towards police headquarters.

Nobody felt like celebrating. Yes, they had got a serial killer off the streets, but not in the way they wanted. Let alone comprehend what was going on.

They booked DSI Crompton in the cells. Watson, Monteith and Lorimer watched as their boss had the ignominy of having his name taken for the records, and fingerprints taken. His personal items, belt, shoelaces and his uniform were taken from him and bagged in a large paper bag. Finally, they saw him being brought down along to the cells, dressed in a paper boiler suit, and watched the door being banged shut behind him.

The next few days were taken up with paperwork. Lots of it. The Independent Office for Police Conduct had come in to take over the case and oversee everything. They interviewed Watson, Monteith, and Lorimer. They had transferred Crompton to a police station out of Ravenswood for his interview and arraignment. Crompton had kept silent throughout. The only words he uttered were, 'No comment.'

Forensic officers had found Littlewood's red book while searching his home. It contained a list of seventeen names. Four had been crossed out, Ronald Freeman, Jackson Davis, Adrian Knowles, and Duncan Healey. The identity of the bloated body in the river, as Mac now could confirm.

Susan Littlewood had been arrested and charged with aiding and abetting the abduction and murders of the four men. In her statement, she blamed everything on her father, saying she'd been scared of him. From getting the job at the prison to help compile the list in the red book. Her father's revenge was not hers anymore. Now, she was on her own.

Of the other thirteen, three names popped out: Billy, Davy and Joseph Clayton. How close had they been to becoming Littlewood's next victims?

The Ravenswood police needed a new Detective Superintendent. Watson knew he'd not yet qualify, not in Matthews' eyes. Rumours had been going around about who it could be. Some experienced copper or an ambitious fast-tracked one barely out of their police nappies?

One morning, while Monteith, Watson, and Lorimer were having a well-earned coffee break, a smiling Matthews walked into the office. With him was a smartly dressed lady in a black pantsuit with a cream blouse. She was carrying a briefcase.

'Gentlemen, if I can have your attention. I would like to introduce you to your new Detective Superintendent, Tanya Wright.'

'Good afternoon, detectives,' Wright said in a crisp voice. 'It's good to meet you finally. I've heard a lot of good things about you all.'

Before they had a chance to reply, Matthews directed their new boss into the now cleared office of DSI Crompton and shut the door.

'*That* I was not expecting.' Monteith stood up and gestured towards the office.

'What, Matthews being kind or the new DSI?' Watson asked.

'Both.'

Matthews came back out of the office and walked straight past them without looking at them.

DSI Wright stood in her office doorway. 'Gentlemen, if you would step this way? It's time for some introductions.'

A MONTH LATER

Monteith was glad his day had finished. Chief Superintendent Matthews had been pressing him again for information on the Russells, but he was getting nowhere with just being a patron of the casino. They kept their business and private lives separate. Trying to make a jerk like Matthews understand that was impossible.

DSI Tanya Wright turned out to be fair but tough, and Monteith, Watson and Lorimer found they could work well with her.

Watson had already signed off and gone into town to meet his wife and children for a meal out.

Monteith, eager to go home as well, left the office ten minutes later. As he walked towards his BMW, he checked his phone. *Just the normal crap*, he thought.

His hand reached for the car door. Two men, dressed in dark clothing, suddenly appeared in front of him.

One of them smashed a right-handed punch into Monteith's face. The force of the punch sent him bouncing off the front of the car next to him. He groaned and stumbled. But before he could get up, a hessian bag was put over his head and his hands were bound behind his back.

'What the hell... Who are you?' Monteith shouted. He screamed as the full force of a kick in the stomach hit him.

He heard a van pull up and doors opening. His attackers lifted him off the ground and threw him into the back of the van. Doors were slammed shut, and the engine revved as the van moved off.

———

Allan Russell watched from his car. The guys were doing their job down to the letter, he thought. Monteith didn't know what hit him as the boys grabbed him and stuffed him into the van. He waited till the van had left the car park before he followed at a safe distance.

'Got you,' he said.

———

Jimmy Russell was sampling one of the finest scotches in his collection, a Highland Park, distilled in 1974 and bottled in 2006. Only one hundred and forty-one bottles had ever been produced. As he leant back in his leather chair, his mobile beeped. It was a text message.

Your package has been collected

THE END

To be continued in book 2 of the Ravenswood Crime Series:
Blood Ties

Acknowledgements

I would like to thank Caroline and Jon at City Stone Publishing for their hard work in publishing this book. They have made me feel very welcome, and I am happy to work with them.

I would also like to thank Ross Greenwood, for the invitation to Dark Side Of Fiction, and for bouncing ideas off his head in regards to the prison parts of this book. To Maureen Davis and Beryl Fielder for their help as BETA readers.

To Kerrie Watson and Kerry Monteith. The original Watson & Monteith. It was a pleasure working with you.

Finally I would like to thank you, the readers. Thank you for purchasing this book, and I hope you have enjoyed it. Please, leave a review on Amazon, Goodreads or any of the other review sites.

Regards,
Tony

About the Author

Tony Millington is the author of the *Ravenswood Crime Series*, currently comprising five books. Set in the fictional city of Ravenswood, DCI Watson and his sidekick, DS Monteith, are the lead detectives of the city's police force.

Prior to writing, Tony spent many years as a civil servant in the MOD, working on local RAF bases. Also, he worked for the local council in Adult and Children's Social Care. He originates from Cheshire, and moved down to Rutland when he was thirteen. He now lives in Cambridgeshire and has been happily married for over twenty-six years; the couple has a son.

Tony volunteers as a facilitator in Peterborough for AMC (Andy's Man Club) charity, a men's suicide prevention charity.

When not writing and walking his Romanian rescue dog, Mira, or catering to the demands of his cat Lucky, you can find Tony rocking out to heavy metal.

Tony Millington on social media:
Facebook: TonyMillingtonAuthor
Twitter: @TonyMillington9

About City Stone Publishing

Indie publisher with a passion for the written word and a heart that beats for authors everywhere

We are an imaginative and enthusiastic indie publisher.

Our ambition is twofold:

To develop outstanding books and work alongside our authors.

To be a beacon of advice and a provider of services for indie authors.

We are not just about the books; we build relationships with our authors. Because we both write, we know what (indie) authors want. That is how we work: in cooperation and partnership with our authors.

From dark and gritty crime thrillers, adventurous fantasy, entertaining women's fiction, and intriguing contemporary novels to interesting and insightful non-fiction and visionary poetry, we publish it all.

Visit our website: citystonepublishing.com

About AMC

ANDYSMANCLUB are a men's suicide prevention charity, offering free-to-attend peer-to-peer support groups across the United Kingdom and online.

Their goal is to end the stigma surrounding men's mental health and help men through the power of conversation.

ANDYSMANCLUB want to eliminate the stigma surrounding mental health and create a judgment-free, confidential space where men can be open about the storms in their lives.

They aim to achieve this through weekly, free-to-attend peer-to-peer support groups for men aged over 18.

#ITSOKAYTOTALK
www.andysmanclub.co.uk

9 781915 399199